I0772955

COME WITH ME

by

Florence Witkop

Copyright © 2024 by Florence Witkop
Published by Winged Publications

Editor: Cynthia Hickey
Book Design by Winged Publications

All rights reserved. No part of this publication may be reproduced, stored in a retrieval system, or transmitted in any form or by any means—electronic, mechanical, photocopying, recording, or otherwise—without the prior written permission of the publisher. The only exception is brief quotations in printed reviews. Piracy is illegal. Thank you for respecting the hard work of this author.

This book is a work of fiction. Names, characters, Places, incidents, and dialogues are either products of the author's imagination or used fictitiously. Any resemblance to actual persons, living or dead, or events is coincidental.

ISBN-13: 978-1-962168-77-9

The road ahead was dark. Too dark. Jude gripped the steering wheel and tried to see enough to keep going but the rain poured down the outside of the windows like a waterfall. The windshield wipers couldn't keep up. We couldn't continue. It would be suicide.

The road curved. Jude slowed but the rain-slicked highway didn't allow for much control so we slid around the curve, gradually slowing to half speed. When it seemed we'd made it safely, a semi-truck appeared from the opposite direction.

The truck loomed closer and closer. Then the worst thing possible happened. It hit a slick spot, went out of control, slid sidewise, and headed across the center line. Towards us.

Not even Jude, the consummate jet pilot, could avoid a collision, not in the rain, not on pavement that resembled black ice more than concrete.

At the last second, he accelerated and powered the SUV until it flew through the night as he pointed it towards the side of the road. We swerved wildly and if he didn't get us past that semi there'd have been a major accident.

But he managed.

When we were safe, he pulled to the side of the road, put on the emergency blinkers, and dropped his head to the steering wheel as the semi continued on down the road. Then he lifted his head and looked through the windshield, staring into the dark and the rain.

"We can't continue." His eyes were bleary from lack of sleep.

"Do we have a choice? Will it let us stop?" Mine were wide with the shock of almost dying.

"We need sleep. Everyone does. Surely whoever – whatever -- is doing this to us will let us get a little rest."

We looked at one another, the same question in both our minds. Would the compulsion that was forcing us to make this journey give us permission to stop? If it did let us stop, where could we spend the night? Were there motels nearby? Was there even a town ahead?

We didn't know the answers to those questions.

In all honesty, we didn't even know *why* we were driving through the night in a storm of epic proportions with rain sluicing along the car. We didn't know *why* we were in such a panic to drive north. Just north.

But we knew we *had* to do it. *Had* to keep going. *Had* to keep heading north. *Had* to get somewhere. *Had* to.

We had no choice in the matter. None at all.

~

Earlier – at least a week earlier, though it could have been more because time became confusing after a while -- an elderly man held a door open for me.

I was charmed as he smiled and tipped his head. I couldn't know what was behind the thoughtful, old-world gesture, but I loved it. It made me feel special. As I passed, he raised his head slightly to meet my look and smiled in an enigmatic way. As if he knew something I didn't and I found that, too, to be charming.

Then he moved towards parts unknown and I entered the building and went in search of my first seminar. I expected to forget all about him in seconds.

I didn't. All during that seminar I mentally blocked out the speaker and instead saw the elderly man. The silver hair that was thick and shiny in a rather long cut. The sparkle in his faded blue eyes. The courtly gestures that had been so unexpected and had made me feel special. And that enigmatic something about him.

I found myself smiling internally while trying to remember to take notes on the finer points of raising puppies that would later become service dogs. Because that's what the convention was about. It was why so many people had converged on the huge building with the large, heavy, carved doors that he'd held open. Service dogs. It was why I was there.

Other than the somewhat unusual topic of service dogs, though, the convention was like all conventions. Loud and chaotic and soon after leaving that first seminar I developed a headache. It appeared full blown as I made my way through the crowded, noisy halls to my next event. I tried to make headway and failed completely.

I pulled the map of the building from my purse and tried to figure where I should be next, checking the map while walking and wishing my head would stop throbbing. Bad move on my part because I walked straight into a solid object. No, I realized, as I studied the object before me. Not an object at all. A person. A man.

Oops.

I turned red and backed up a couple feet and was about to turn away and disappear in the crowd when my victim reached out and grabbed my hand. I froze but he held me lightly. Nothing nasty even though I'd almost run him over, though judging from the solid bulk before me, it would have taken a lot more than me to knock him off his feet. Two of me, at least. Or three.

"Are you okay?" *He* was worried about *me*? I ran into him, not the other way around. But he chose tact and said, "We had a collision."

I nodded while avoiding eye contact. I was that embarrassed. But even through my eyelashes I could tell he was tallish, well built and didn't seem angry. The not angry part was the important thing. I cautiously raised my head until I could see him straight-on. "I'm sorry. It was my fault."

"No it wasn't. I bumped into you." He looked around and kind of hauled me out of the flow of traffic because if we stayed where we were we'd both be knocked sidewise. "Or maybe we were pushed into each other by this veritable sea of humanity." A sudden grin split his face. "Though if either of us had become unbalanced we wouldn't have fallen because it's too crowded to allow for a decent fall."

Not only was he tallish and well built, he had a

sense of humor and was nice. Decent. Trying to make me feel better and since he seemed to be waiting for me to say something, I said the first thing that came into my mind and that was about service dogs because it was a convention for people who dealt with them. "Do you train service dogs?"

He shook his head as a woman in a hurry knocked me towards the wall on her way to somewhere but he grabbed me before I hit. His reaction time was amazing, his arms strong. "Nope."

"Then are you with someone who's looking for one?"

"Nope again."

The crowd thinned as people got to wherever they were headed for their next seminar. But it was still busy and the hum of talk made it necessary to step close to be heard. "But surely you have something to do with service dogs or you'd not be here." I was becoming curious.

"I do not deal with them nor do I know anything about them." He expertly diverted a couple who almost plowed into us as he kind of hovered over me protectively. I was grateful. "But the people I work for do know a lot and they are big donors. They were invited. So here I am."

"Oh. You're here on business."

"Yes, but I have nothing to do until they are ready to leave and that'll be when the convention ends. Three days. So, I decided to look around and see what the whole thing is about." He checked both ways along the hall and when he saw the coast was clear he moved away from the wall and I followed.

"There seems to be a lot to learn but in all honesty

I'm ready for a break even though it's still early. I need my morning coffee." His eyebrows quirked in a question. "Want to join me and we can compare war stories? If you don't have someplace to be."

"I'm signed up for another seminar. But I'm not sure I'll go. I have a headache." Which was getting worse by the second.

He looked around the hall that was semi-empty by then. "You are already late. Everyone will look at you when you enter the room and that'll make your headache worse." He grinned like a kid playing hooky. "I have nothing to do and the day is just starting. What say you come with me and I'll treat you to coffee and aspirin. I have some with me."

I didn't have aspirin and he did, and I wanted some. So I looked along the corridor and momentarily closed my eyes against the headache and said, "Sure. Let's go."

An hour later the headache was less and I knew his name was Jude Fielding and he was a corporate jet pilot who'd flown in a bevy of business types who were considering giving a considerable amount of money to help raise and train service dogs.

In that time over coffee, he'd also learned a lot about me. "You are Diedre Brown, accountant, and you raise and socialize puppies in your spare time until they are ready to attend doggie school." He tipped his head exactly as the elderly man had done earlier and I wondered whether the gesture on his part was courtesy or curiosity. Either way, I liked it. "And where did you stash your current puppy so you could attend the convention?"

"I'm between puppies at the moment."

I looked beyond him and was surprised to see the elderly man with the silver hair enter the coffee bar. The man who'd held the door for me earlier. Our eyes met and he nodded and smiled and I couldn't help doing the same. Jude turned around to see who I was smiling at. "You know him?"

I told him what had happened. "And he remembers you and you remember him after just a few seconds at the entrance?" He examined the elderly man. "Though now I see him, I think I might have talked with him earlier. Just like you. At the east door, right?" I nodded as the elderly man turned his smile towards Jude. It was both polite and genuine. "Yes, he's the man I saw. I remember now, just like you remembered. That smile is impossible to forget."

"He seemed nice."

Jude agreed that he was nice as he and the elderly man nodded to each other. Then Jude turned back to me and the elderly man ordered a coffee that he took somewhere else while Jude and I refilled ours and took them outside and sat on the steps of the convention building because it was the lovely kind of day that promised to make the rest of my headache disappear. And it did.

When our coffee was gone, we didn't go our separate ways. Instead, we spent the rest of that day together. Not for any reason and not because of some sudden inner connection. Rather I'd decided I didn't want to risk another headache and neither of us had anything special to do so we decided to do nothing together and the rest of that day turned out to be as lovely as our time sitting on the steps had been.

I decided Jude Fielding might be former military.

He had the erect posture, short haircut and general air of competence that speaks of military service. He was also gorgeous in a tall-dark-and-handsome kind of way and I enjoyed the looks from other women who thought Jude and I were actually an item. It was fun and laughable, relaxing and bubbly.

The day passed quickly. All too soon it was time to return to my motel and for Jude to go wherever he went while waiting to fly the corporate types back to wherever they came from. As we exited the building and separated, we looked back and saw the silver-haired man again. He waved at us with that memorable smile and we waved back because he was a nice man and because we both felt like waving and smiling and the elderly man gave us a good excuse to do so.

In my motel room I downloaded some work for a client who needed his books done immediately. Bookkeeping is like that and when you are self-employed it happens oftener than would seem possible. But I finished eventually and fell asleep quickly and easily and awoke the next morning ready for the second day of the convention. The day when I'd actually attend the seminars I'd signed up for.

CHAPTER 2

I didn't attend any seminars the next morning, either, and I didn't even feel guilty because spending the day with a man completely charming and friendly and interesting was much better than listening to someone drone on about how to raise the puppies I'd been raising long enough that I could probably teach him a few things.

That man wasn't Jude Fielding. He was the man I'd met at the entrance the first day of the convention and that second day happened almost exactly the same as the first, with a courteous nod of his head while he swept the door open for me. But this time I stopped and smiled broadly and was rewarded by a similar smile as he waved me through.

I don't know why I spoke. Perhaps because Jude and I had talked about him the previous day. Perhaps because his old-world courtesies had got to me. How many men treat women like that now? "Thank you."

He nodded. "You're welcome, lovely lady."

I blushed. Yes, I actually blushed. "Do you open the door for everyone?" Perhaps it was his job?

He shook his head. "Only for the truly nice people." His words were followed by a deprecating chuckle. "Which is almost everyone so perhaps it's as you suggest."

The door remained open, but I hesitated. "Are you some kind of gallant knight?"

He let the door close by itself as he straightened, eyes gleaming with intelligence and the kind of sunshine that had sent my headache away the previous day. "I can't pretend to be noble but good manners are never out of style."

"And you have them in abundance." I'd been curious about Jude the day before. I was curious now about this elderly silver-haired man. "Do you train service dogs?" If he did, he must be one of the best, the kind whose dogs were always polite and courteous and caring.

"No. I can't pretend to be as gifted as those who do. But I am impressed with everyone here." He cocked his head exactly as I remembered him doing before. "This place is full of people who love and care for living beings of a different species." He paused and his eyes shone with passion. "Such people are special. That's why I'm here. I find such people intriguing and I want to be around them for a brief moment." What he said next sealed my fate for the entirety of that morning. "People like you, Diedre Brown."

"You know my name." A statement not a question.

"You impressed me yesterday. I asked around." His eyebrows furrowed in a question." I hope you don't mind."

"Of course I don't mind." He could be an axe murderer with a killer smile for all I knew but I returned that smile with one of my own. "And what's your name if you don't mind telling me?"

"Lourdes Jones at your service." He swept low in a bow and the two of us entered the building together as meetings, seminars and classes flew out of my mind because being with Lourdes Jones would be far, far more entertaining and when the convention ended, I'd have a special memory to take home with me. No doubt about it. He was that charismatic.

As it turned out I only spent the morning with him. During that time, though, as we wandered the halls and took in the displays and enjoyed the ambience of a convention of people who loved dogs, I saw Jude Fielding now and then. He always seemed to be headed in the opposite direction but we waved as we passed.

"You know him?" Lourdes asked. "Am I keeping you from meeting a friend?" He patted my hand. "I don't want to steal you away from anyone important."

"Just someone I was with yesterday." Impulsively I told him what Jude had said. "He recognized you as someone he'd met in passing. Just as I did."

"And he was nice?"

I thought a moment. "Very nice. He's a pilot. He flew some people here."

His response was to watch Jude disappear around a corner. "Another interest of mine. Flight."

"Then you'd enjoy meeting him."

"I'm sure you're right about that."

And so the morning went. I expected we'd spend the rest of the day together. We had lunch in the crowded café on one side of the building where Jude and I had had lunch the previous day. Then with a dip of his head Lourdes Jones said he had to leave. "Something has come up, I'm afraid. Something unexpected."

"I hope it's not a problem."

"No problem. I have an errand to run and unfortunately it can't wait. I apologize."

"That's alright. I should attend at least one seminar today."

We parted and I looked up the afternoon list of seminars and chose one about sick puppies. When the session ended, I knew when to call the vet immediately as opposed to simply hugging a puppy and waiting a bit in case it was just lonely.

But as I left the seminar and wondered what to do with the remaining day I glanced up and saw Lourdes Jones. And Jude Fielding. They were together, wandering much as Lourdes and I had wandered that morning.

Then I remembered. I'd mentioned that Jude was a pilot and Lourdes had mentioned being interested in flight. I'd been dumped in favor of a guy who knew about planes and I chuckled all the way to my next seminar, one with real, live dogs that showed off their well-trained selves to oohs and aahs from myself and everyone else in the room.

When I returned to my motel room that night, I wondered what would happen on the third and last day of the convention. So far, I'd met two very interesting men and had skipped more informative seminars than I'd attended.

The last day, though, wasn't to be so much for seminars and workshops as it was for speeches and the service dogs themselves roaming the halls with their trainers and showing what they could do and how well they could handle themselves. It promised to be a full and rather interesting day with or without male companionship.

I'd never have guessed I'd spend that last day with both men, Lourdes Jones and Jude Fielding, though I would have guessed if I'd known what would happen when I arrived in the morning at the building with the huge, heavy, ornate doors that were difficult to open.

Lourdes Jones was the entrance except this time he wasn't alone. Jude Fielding stood beside him as they talked animatedly but not so much so that Lourdes forgot to open the door for me.

I laughed as he swung it open and watched as he swept low in a bow and called me 'lovely lady' as he'd done the previous day and I couldn't help but feel special. He might have been acting but it worked. I blushed and stopped and thanked him for being such a gentleman.

He took my hand and placed it on his arm as people did hundreds of years ago and steered us through the open doorway with Jude Fielding following and catching my attention with an expression that said it had already been arranged that the three of us would spend the day together.

Sometime during the day Lourdes Jones repeated what he'd said that first time we spoke. "I'm impressed that so many people care about living beings of a different species. I think such people are special. In fact, I know they are." He looked straight at me. Through me. "People like you, Diedre Brown." Then he turned to Jude. "And also you, Jude Fielding."

Jude put up his hands in protest. "I don't train service dogs. I don't do anything with dogs or cats or any other species. I just fly planes."

"Jets, to be specific," Lourdes said. "Which is just

as special in its own way as caring for a different species. Without pilots there'd be no flights and without flights how would anyone get around and see places other than where they were born and meet people and other species different from themselves?" He shook his head as if this was an astonishing fact. "They wouldn't, that's what. So the way I see it, pilots and puppy caretakers are both special and I'm privileged to spend this day with the both of you."

Jude and I looked at each other over Lourdes' head and didn't know quite how to respond so we remained silent but the praise circled through my body and settled in some part of me that said it was a beautiful day that I'd remember forever and Lourdes was the reason.

Though, as I inspected the luscious, all-male Jude, I admitted that he was just as memorable though in a different way. I'd think about him a lot in the coming months. I knew I would. And I'd drool. Not that it would do any good. He'd have flown away in his jet and I'd be back home doing other people's books and raising puppies.

As the day passed both Jude and I realized something. We didn't speak about it in front of Lourdes but it was in the looks we passed between us over his head. The elderly, silver-haired man was playing matchmaker and we were the couple he was trying in every way possible to get together.

When Lourdes went to get a refill of coffee Jude's eyebrows rose and he said, "Do you suppose he does this often?"

"I hope not but if it's a habit of his I doubt anyone is insulted because he's such an all-around nice guy."

"I agree and if it's okay with you we can cater to

his fantasy and pretend to be a couple for the remainder of the day."

"It will make him feel good." Jude nodded and it was agreed and Jude took my hands in his as Lourdes returned and saw us together and beamed beneficently.

We spent the rest of the day like that, hand in hand, following Lourdes through the halls admiring the service dogs and their handlers. Lourdes clearly loved them as much as he enjoyed playing matchmaker. Several times he repeated what he'd said earlier. "I find it amazing and wonderful that so many people connect on so many levels with a species different than their own." He shook his head in admiration. "It's absolutely wonderful."

We were sure that what Lourdes Jones did later, as the convention wound down, was deliberate. We were in the cafe on the side of the building and he'd insisted on treating us to a glass of iced tea. When he returned with three tall, frosted glassed and handed one to each of us, he took a long drink of his and said, "I do apologize but I must see to something. I hope you don't mind me cutting out a bit early. Do you?" We insisted we were fine with him leaving. "But you two mustn't separate just because I must go somewhere." He put his hands on ours and joined them together. "Because you make such a lovely couple."

Our eyes met as we silently agreed to go along with his matchmaking for a bit longer so we left our hands together until we had to separate in order to drink our tea as Lourdes glowed with happiness because he'd created a loving couple. Us.

The tea was excellent. Beyond excellent. Our looks met still again with a silent agreement that Lourdes

Jones knew his iced tea. We drank every last drop until Lourdes set his own empty glass on the table and left, turning for one last wave before disappearing.

Jude said it first. "I flew in a bunch of executives. I came to the convention because I had nothing better to do while waiting to fly them back." He raised his empty glass. It became a prism for the sunshine coming through the window and created a rainbow that danced on the nearby wall. "But it turned out to be much more." His eyes narrowed as he considered me. "And you and Lourdes Jones are the reasons. I'm glad I came. I'm glad I met Lourdes. And I'm glad I met you, Diedre Brown, even if we aren't quite the romantic duo Lourdes thinks we are."

I raised my glass too. It didn't catch the sunlight but our glasses clinked in a satisfying way as we toasted the convention and ourselves. "Me too. I'll remember these three days for a long time and the service dogs are only part of the reason."

Lourdes would have been pleased with Jude's next action. He leaned close and kissed me. It was a light kiss on the cheek but three days ago such an act would have been unthinkable. At the moment it was not only acceptable, it was perfect and I was sure Lourdes would have smiled.

CHAPTER 3

On the way out of the café we asked for refills of the wonderful, iced tea to take with us. "Sugar or zero calorie sweetener?"

We chose sugar because that was most likely what Lourdes had chosen. The server took our glasses and gave us our tea in Styrofoam cups. We sipped it on the way out of the building. It was good but not the same as Lourdes had brought. Jude shrugged. "The server must be new."

"Hasn't yet learned the finer points of making iced tea like the one who made our first glasses." We laughed at the world of work that had both experienced employees and newbies and you got whichever was available at the moment. We pushed open the huge, heavy, ornate doors and left the convention building for the last time and headed for the parking lot.

I thought we both lingered longer than necessary as we reached a place where we'd go our separate ways but it could have been my imagination. There was no reason Jude would be reluctant to see me go, though, as I found my car I admitted to myself that I wished for a reason to prolong our leave taking. Because I wanted him to stay in my life longer. As long as possible. The attraction was that strong.

But he was a pilot and I was a bookkeeper and our paths would never cross again and I might as well get used to that fact. So, I turned away from him, climbed into my car and made the long drive home.

When I entered the house, I had turned into my own little corner of peace and tranquility, it felt odd. Not scary or uncomfortable. Not wrong, either. Not even close to wrong. The feeling wasn't anything I could define. But I somehow felt as if I wasn't the same person who'd left a few days earlier.

I stared at myself in the mirror in the bathroom as I cleaned up after the drive and told myself that of course I wasn't the same person because look what had happened during those days. They'd been filled with two interesting men and a lot of wonderful service dogs. It would be strange if I wasn't changed.

I had a busy rest of the day. I caught up on as much work as possible, promised myself a busier next day of still more catch-up, and went to bed much later than usual. I expected to fall asleep instantly and I did.

But I didn't sleep well.

I had dreams.

Not nightmares because they weren't frightening or confusing. In fact, they were pleasant and very precise and that was odd because dreams aren't normally detailed. At least my dreams weren't. They tended to be blurry and indistinct.

But my dream that night was as detailed as if I was watching a rolodex display of pictures of a place I'd never been or read about or even seen in a movie but the pictures were vivid down to sunlight filtering through tall, old-growth trees and flashing off ripples on a wind-ruffled lake.

It was a lovely place wherever it was. Somewhere up north, perhaps, because the trees were evergreens? Though as to that, I decided when I awoke and went over my dream, many southern areas also have evergreens. But the lake had the crystal clarity typical of northern lakes so I thought that was where the dream place must be. And the dream had felt northern.

Except dreams aren't real and why was I thinking about it as if it was? It was a dream, just a dream, and the only thing odd about it was that I remembered it so well the next morning. Every second of it. The blue and gray birds flying through the sky against fluffy white clouds. The doe and fawn drinking at the edge of the lake and then lingering a while before returning to the forest. I shook my head in puzzlement as I made coffee and turned on my computer to begin the day's work.

Then I stopped because someone called me and the call was from somewhere in my house. I panicked and had to force myself to check each room until I was sure there was no one there and decided it had been my imagination. So I shook my head, decided I had an overactive imagination, and went back to my work and concentrated on payroll.

But if it was my imagination why didn't it stop? Because it didn't. Someone – some voice -- kept calling my name. I knew it was imaginary but it continued. The voice called again and then still again. I finally gave up getting anything accomplished and pushed the bookkeeping aside, determined to get to the bottom of whatever was happening.

I closed my eyes and concentrated on listening because by then I'd decided my first thought was right after all and someone was in my house and playing a very unfunny joke on me and if I listened hard enough, I might figure out who it was and deal with them severely. But no matter how hard I tried I couldn't find the person belonging to the voice or recognize who it was.

As I listened intently, though, I realized it wasn't a normal voice, though precisely how it was abnormal I couldn't figure. A computerized voice? Maybe but maybe not. An actor that was adept with accents? Again, I couldn't know for sure or what accent it might be.

In fact, no matter how hard I tried I couldn't pinpoint what about the voice was odd. Just that something was and that made it impossible for me to know who might be doing something nasty to me.

The upshot of all that concentration on the voice meant I got nothing done that day and went to bed knowing I'd better get a good night's sleep because the next day I'd have two days' worth of work to do and I'd better get it done because a business was counting on me for their payroll.

But I didn't get much sleep because once again I dreamed and it was that same dream. Except this time there was an added element. Jude Fielding, the jet pilot, was in my dream and he was looking at me in a way he'd never done at the convention, rather in the way I'd wished he'd looked at me. Wanted him to look at me. Hoped he would. But he hadn't.

The man had definitely got to me if I was now including him in my dreams.

Then it got worse. In my dream he not only looked at me in that special man-woman way, he spoke in a husky, emotion filled voice. "Do you like the lake as much as I do?" In my dream I nodded and his eyes crinkled in a way that made me stop breathing. "Then let's go for a swim because the water is crystal clear, though it might be a bit cold."

In my dream he dipped a hand in the lake and flicked drops of water that I caught with one hand and he was right. It was perfect, though cool. And I pulled off my shirt to reveal a swimsuit beneath and headed for the water beside Jude who was doing the same.

What magic had the guy wrought on me at that convention that I not only dreamed of him, I'd inserted him into my dreams and they were getting progressively more and more romantic. Pretty soon in my dreams we'd be making out. And more.

Fortunately, I woke up before our dream selves reached that point. I sat straight up in bed, threw the covers off, and stared into the darkness.

This was crazy. I was crazy.

Then, in the middle of the night in my bed, I heard that voice again, the strange, unrecognizable voice that wasn't normal but I couldn't figure out how it was abnormal. But this time it only said one word but that word wasn't my name. It said, "Come." Then it repeated that single word. "Come."

Then the voice faded away and I was suddenly cold and felt very alone in the house I'd always loved and felt comfortable in. I hugged myself and decided I'd better get myself straightened out if I didn't want to go insane and spend the rest of my life cowering in my own home and listening to imaginary voices.

It wouldn't take long to return to normal, I told myself. I was tough. I'd push that darn voice back to wherever it came from. I could do it. After all, it was a temporary dream thing and dreams aren't real even if it did seem real. Feel real. I could return to my normal self. I could! It would just require a bit of effort.

I breathed deeply, lay back down, pulled the covers tight and closed my eyes, determined to sleep without dreams for the rest of the night. That didn't happen. Instead, I spent the rest of the night dreaming that same dream. Over and over again and Jude Fielding was always a part of it.

Just before dawn, though, before the sun rose, another element was added. A new and different element.

A light appeared deep in that dream forest that waxed and waned. If it disappeared entirely, it always reappeared. And never could I see what caused the light or exactly where in the forest it was located other than that it seemed to be near a hill.

In the morning, I woke up sweating and exhausted. This had to stop. So I went shopping and came home with every over-the-counter sleeping pill I could find. There was no doubt about it. I would sleep that night and I wouldn't dream.

Didn't happen. I still dreamed that same repetitious dream and every time Jude was in it, smiling at me and inviting me to join him to do something. Swim. Walk along a forest trail. Climb a hill and survey the wilderness. Always Jude. And the two of us were always doing something together. Something romantic.

In the morning, I was more exhausted than the previous day but I dragged myself to my computer and worked without stopping until I was caught up. I sent the results to my clients and staggered to the couch where I dropped into the deep cushions and just stared at nothing.

As I lay there wondering if I'd sleep that night, I heard that unrecognizable voice that couldn't possibly exist but did. It repeated that single word of earlier. "Come."

Then the message changed. It added my name. "Come, Diedre Brown. Come."

In total frustration, I picked up one of the couch pillows and threw it at the wall. The act felt so good that I repeated it with all the couch pillows and the ones on the chairs. When there were no more pillows to throw, I picked them up and carefully replaced them and wondered what I was thinking to have done such a stupid thing. I wondered what I was becoming. What was wrong with me. And I knew I had to fix me.

CHAPTER 4

The first item on my agenda to fix me was to see a doctor. I told him I was having trouble sleeping and could he prescribe something? He did and it worked for a night. Then it didn't work so I went back and said I needed a different prescription and he referred me to a psychiatrist. That was the end of my seeking medical help. I refused to consider myself insane. At least I refused to admit it officially.

But I still had the dreams and when I checked myself in the mirror, I looked ten years older than the previous day. When I met another accountant, I often worked with for lunch she said I looked like death warmed over. Later, at a business meeting a client said I looked overworked. Both silently backed away from me as if I had the plague.

I had to do something or I'd lose my business.

The next time I heard the voice, in the middle of the day, it truly scared me. It spoke entire sentences. "Time is passing quickly, Diedre. There isn't much time left. You must come soon." The voice was gentle but I wasn't fooled, not even in the dream. It wasn't a suggestion. It was an order.

That night the voice elaborated on the message.

"You are one of two and you are both ready. So come, both of you. Come now. Come immediately."

The following day I tried to push away the terror those words brought. I concentrated fiercely on bookkeeping because I had a business to run that required my full and absolute attention. Numbers are like that. You'd better get them right.

But after two nights of being given an order that had to be imaginary but that scared the life out of me anyway, I admitted that the bookkeeping – and my life -- weren't going well. Something had to be done.

I called a couple bookkeepers I knew and distributed my clients among them until such time as I could once more do a decent job. I said I was sure it would be soon but they insisted it wasn't a problem. "Take all the time you need. Get healthy." I hadn't told them what my health problem was, just that I had one and I was sure the friend I'd had lunch with had already spread the gossip about me. So they weren't surprised.

Then another weird thing was added to the weirdness that was my life. But it wasn't just a new or different dream. It was strange and odd but it had to be connected to the dreams somehow. Had to be because it was as weird as my dreams.

The new thing couldn't be easily described because it was pure emotion and emotion is hard to describe. To understand. It wasn't a dream. It was a feeling.

It was an emotion and it was so elemental that it quickly became pure need, a compulsion so strong that it set my teeth on edge until my whole body thrummed with it. As the hours passed with me going from one room to another in an attempt to get away from it and then out into the yard where I tried gardening without success, I realized I couldn't ignore it no matter what I did or how hard I tried. It was a part of me whether I wished it or not. Had become a part of me without me realizing it or knowing how it had happened.

Most important, though, it was in charge of me.

The compulsion told me to climb into my car and drive until I could feel in real life the coolness of the wind soughing through that richly green forest and the warmth of the sun on my body that I'd felt in my dreams. It was so strong that I needed – absolutely *needed* -- to smell the piney woods and enjoy the ambiance of the tiny sand beach along the shore of the lake I'd never seen in real life and I also felt a desperate need to feel the water of that unknown lake on my body.

I needed to experience those things. Needed to. I felt like my life depended on it and the need grew stronger until it was a basic, gut-level, life-or-death compulsion so great that I absolutely had to experience those things, not just dream about them. I needed to *go* to where those things were. To get in my car, leave my home, and just drive until I found them.

The compulsion told me to go north. To drive in a northerly direction and just keep driving until I found what I was looking for. But of course, I couldn't do that. I had a business and a life. And I wasn't insane.

But the compulsion grew so strong that my life fell apart. I couldn't sleep. I forgot to eat. I didn't bathe properly or shop for the necessities of daily life. I didn't clean my house. I didn't do any of the usual things people do. Eventually I knew I had to bring myself back to reality or I'd not survive.

I decided my first step in reclaiming my life would

be to go shopping. Not just shopping, I decided, it would be a major shopping-as-therapy trip complete with a leisurely meal with waitresses and a decent, healthy, gourmet meal at a sit-down restaurant where I'd be surrounded by normal people and would get some nutrition into me.

So I got in my car and managed to drive to the largest shopping mall in the city instead of immediately turning north as the compulsion wanted me to do.

North. It wanted me to go north because that was where I'd find the lake and the forest and the rest of the dream stuff. But somehow, I went to the mall. I shook from head to toe with the effort of resisting the urge to go north and I was proud of myself as I looked for a decent restaurant where I'd begin my return to normalcy.

I was doing it. I was resisting the compulsion.

I headed for an area of restaurants interspersed with motels that catered to travelers in addition to locals having lunch with coworkers and clients. I saw a nice-looking restaurant and started to turn into the parking lot.

I didn't. Instead, I drove past it because I suddenly couldn't turn the steering wheel to enter the parking lot. Couldn't. My muscles burned with effort but I couldn't do it. I swore in frustration but passed the restaurant anyway.

After that I passed two more restaurants without being able to turn into their parking lots either. Panic began to well up in me. Then, as I was beginning to believe my whole therapy type expedition would be a failure, I noticed a smallish family restaurant next to the first motel off the interstate. I decided to try one last time to turn into a restaurant parking lot. And I did.

I easily turned into their small parking lot and turned off the engine and climbed out of my car and looked at the restaurant. How was this cozy looking place different from the other restaurants I'd not been able to access? Why could I park here when I hadn't been able to park anywhere else? I didn't know.

But time was passing, so I pushed open the door and went into the restaurant proper, grabbed a menu from the stack on the counter and looked for a table. And stopped. Stared. And stared some more as my mouth dropped open in complete surprise as just ahead of me I saw the man from my dreams.

"Jude Fielding?"

His back was to me and he was holding a menu and looking for a table. He heard me. Turned. Saw me. Was as surprised to see me as I was to see him.

"Diedre Brown? What are you doing in this part of the world?" He was dressed casually and looked tired.

"What brought you here?" I countered with a question of my own to give me time to come up with an answer that wouldn't get me sent to the nearest asylum.

We sat at the same table without discussion. Of course we did. We both showed up at the same restaurant in the middle of nowhere on the same day. An amazing coincidence.

"You seem tired," he said as we stared at one another across the table like boxers seeking each other's weak spot, each wondering about the other while not answering the other's questions.

I didn't want him to know what I'd been through even as I couldn't imagine why he was acting the same way I was. Cagey. Furtive. Nor could I figure why he looked as tired as I did.

"Been busy flying executives around the world?" A semi-acceptable conversational gambit that went with his tired look.

"I'm on vacation."

"Because they've kept you so busy you need a break?"

He shook his head. "Actually, it's been slow. The last trip was for the service dog convention."

"And you're tired?" Surprise made me blurt it out. "From that one trip a while back?"

He slumped. "Not from work. It's –" He looked one way and then another. "It's complicated." He looked me over thoughtfully for a long time and changed the topic without answering. "So what's your excuse? Why are you tired and don't try to say you aren't. You look like you could sleep for a week."

I spoke without thinking. "I would if it wasn't for the nightmares." I shook my head. "Not nightmares. Dreams, but the result is the same. Little sleep." That sounded reasonably normal. Everyone has dreams.

"You too?" Astonishment lit up his face. "I'm not the only one having dreams?" We stared at one another until he asked quietly, "If you don't mind my asking, just what are your dreams about?"

The waitress came for our order. We didn't notice her until she cleared her throat and then we scrambled to order something from the menu. She left with identical orders because after I ordered the first thing on the menu, a rack of ribs, Jude said he wanted the same.

I was sure it was because he was too spooked to muster the ability to read the menu and not because he loved ribs. He hadn't even looked at the menu. He'd been too busy staring at me.

"So, what are your dreams about?" He leaned way too casually over the table until hardly any space separated us but his eyes were intent, his nostrils flared, his words a little too carefully spoken and he held me in thrall with a kind of magnetism as if we were connected by a rope – or a filament – or magic -- as he waited for my answer.

I squirmed. Looked over his shoulder. Wished I had a logical answer but I didn't. "Mostly I dream of a place."

The table was small, we were so close I could feel his breath stop and see his eyes widen at my words. He cleared his throat. "Your dream is of a lake in a forest." It wasn't a question. It was a statement of fact that he knew to be true. "It is. I know it is."

My hands moved restlessly on the table, this way and that, unable to stay still though the rest of me couldn't move as I said, "And there's a light somewhere beyond where we are standing."

"You say 'we' because we are both in the dream." He took my hands in his own and we stared as our fingers laced together. "You and me." He exhaled slowly. "Am I right?"

I nodded. "Both of us. Sometimes swimming. Sometimes just being in the forest."

"Sometimes in a canoe? Do you ever see us in a canoe?"

I nodded again. "It's in one of the dreams. A birchbark canoe."

"And in one dream a doe and her fawn come to drink at the lake."

Words petered out and we simply stared at one

another until the waitress returned with two orders of ribs. We waited until she left before continuing. "We are dreaming the same dream."

"Which is why we are both tired. The dreams won't let us sleep."

"And we were told that there are two of us." His voice was grim and I nodded. "Though we weren't told what we are supposed to be two of." He pointed from himself to me and back again. "But it's clear to me now that we are the two the dreams are about. You and me."

He took a deep breath. I could see him decide to go for it, to make a fool of himself if necessary in order to know the extent of the truth that now lay between us like a dark pool of unknown depth. "It's because of those dreams that I took some vacation time and am headed north."

I was shocked. "You're following the compulsion?" I'd said it. I'd used the word. Compulsion. In saying it, I'd accepted that he, too, felt the need to go north. Just north. And he didn't argue with me. He thought of it the same way, I could see in his eyes that he did. As a compulsion.

"It's the only way to regain a normal life. Find the origin of the dreams, look it in the eye, and then stare it into nothingness."

"I'm fighting it."

"Good luck with that."

I took an exploratory bite of the ribs. It was why I was there, after all, to have a normal experience in a normal restaurant. They might have been good ribs. I didn't know.

But the fact that I was there for lunch raised a question. Was I at this specific restaurant by choice or because at some level I'd been compelled to come here because it's where I'd meet Jude? I didn't ask Jude because I didn't have to. I knew the answer. We both did.

We ate for long moments in silence, looking at one another every so often and then looking away. Finally, Jude put his silverware down, lay his hands on the table and waited until I looked at him and when that happened he dared me not to look away. Then he said, simply, "Come with me. Let's find the source together."

The world stopped. I was sure other people in the restaurant continued with their meals and conversations and whatever else they were doing but I didn't hear any of it. Didn't see it. I only saw Jude's hands on the table, large and strong and male and the only voice I heard was his voice telling me to join him. "Are you saying I should just give up? Give in to it?"

"It's not giving up. It's finding out what this thing that's driving us insane is about. It's getting to the core of the thing. Going where it wants us to go so we can confront it and end it forever."

"What if it doesn't work out that way?"

"Then that's the chance we'll take." He took both my hands in his and once again willed me not to look away. He was unafraid and was strong in his belief that this was the right thing to do. I wished I had his confidence. I held his hands tight and prayed for his strength to flow into me and tell me whether I should stay home or go with him.

"Okay." I said it. I committed to what he was doing. To joining him. "I'll come with you."

He squeezed my hands and then dropped them.

Without his hands covering mine the room turned cool and fear pressed in on me once again.

I wanted to reach out and hold his hands once more and regain the strength I'd not realized until that moment he was giving me. But I didn't. Instead, I finished my meal as the world came back into focus slowly, sound by sound, person by person. When the waitress came to ask if we wanted dessert, I was able to talk with her and tell her we didn't. Because we had something we had to do and had best get going. She understood.

We decided Jude would follow me home and wait while I contacted the bookkeepers who were helping with my clients to let them know I'd be gone for an uncertain period and to pack practically my entire wardrobe because we didn't know where we'd end up and what the weather would be like. I also included my passport because Jude had brought his. When I was finally ready the only things left in my closet were the dressy outfits I wore to business consults, weddings, and upscale lunches with friends.

When I was done, every suitcase I owned was full and every coat was in a pile and when they were added to Jude's luggage, the back of his SUV was packed with little space for anything more.

Then I just sat at the kitchen table and stared out the window at the yard I'd enjoyed ever since renting the house I called home with the fence that kept puppies safe and the picnic table I sat at whenever the weather was nice and the apple tree I sprayed with insecticide each spring so I could enjoy apples in the autumn. Then I visited my next-door neighbor, the one who always kept my key when I went somewhere.

"How long will you be gone, dearie?"

"I don't know."

I was saved from further explanations when she glanced at Jude, who sat beside me with a closed expression. She tried to read him and failed and finally asked, "Family stuff?"

I nodded because that was as good a reason for an extended time away as any. "You do what you have to do, dearie. I'll watch your house and when you come back you come over and get your key and if you want to talk, I'll be here to listen."

I thanked her, grateful she'd made assumptions about why I was leaving and so didn't ask questions. Then I got into Jude's SUV, gave my rented but much-loved house a long, somber look and turned away as he pulled onto the street and turned north. It was late afternoon by the time we got started so I didn't expect to go far that day. Not far enough to know where we were headed or even to get a good start.

The first part of the trip was easy. We wove through the streets of my small city until we reached the freeway. We pulled onto the north-bound half of the divided highway and Jude started driving, keeping pace with traffic as I enjoyed the passing scenery because the release of stress that came with no longer fighting the compulsion and, instead, giving in to it was so great that it felt more like heading for a holiday weekend at one of the several tourist destinations north of the city than going on a wild goose chase for reasons unknown. I grinned and glanced at Jude in the driver's seat.

He grinned back. He, too, felt the release of tension achieved by doing what the compulsion wanted. And, in a warped and odd way, we were on an adventure.

Those tourist destinations we were headed towards consisted of resorts and motels near a state park with all the touristy fun things families could do on vacation. We drove until evening cast long shadows over the countryside though it was later than it appeared because it was summer and the days were at peak length. As we reached the first motel, Jude started to turn in. And didn't. Instead, he passed it by, a frown marring his face.

"What's wrong?"

"I can't do it."

"The compulsion?" He nodded and fear started somewhere in me.

We passed three motels before we came to one he could turn into. It was much later and was full dark by the time we went inside. Jude asked if there were two rooms available and was told there were not but there was one we could rent.

Jude's raised eyebrows asked if we could share a room and I nodded that we could. He turned back to the clerk and we were given that room. But when Jude gave the man his name and credit card, the clerk frowned. "I don't need this. You already have a room booked."

"No, we don't." Jude was confused. We both were.

The clerk insisted we did and showed us the reservation. "It's paid for and everything."

"Who paid for it?

The clerk tried to find out. "It's a business card, that's all I know. Some business from up north. It doesn't give the name of the business."

I wanted to leave. I was sure Jude did too. But we were there, we knew we'd not be able to stop anywhere else because the compulsion wouldn't let us and we were tired. So, Jude accepted the room. One room and since we'd planned to share one anyway, we could share the one reserved for us. Surely there would be two beds because most motel rooms had two.

"Is there somewhere to eat nearby?"

The clerk said nothing would be open that late but the restaurant connected with the motel could provide sandwiches if that was okay with us. We said it was and were promised they'd be brought to our room.

We rolled our suitcases to the assigned room and went inside and simply sat on the one bed it held and knew we'd both sleep well even if we did have to share not only a room but a bed. It was huge, a king sized one, so it would be okay.

The sandwiches were filling, a meal, and we agreed that in the morning we'd find a grocery store and buy sandwich stuff and drinks and a cooler to keep them in. Just in case the compulsion wouldn't let us stop for meals.

"Surely whoever is behind it knows we must eat."

"Best to be prepared if it won't let us stop."

"We need to sleep and it provided a motel room. So, it must also know we need to eat." He grinned suddenly and the day was brighter for it. "But with one room and one bed either the entity behind the compulsion is really cheap or else it thinks we are married."

I giggled, almost gagging on my sandwich. Soon Jude was laughing instead of just grinning and we finished the sandwiches and took turns showering in the adjoining bath and then we each laid out clothes for the next day and climbed into that huge bed.

Jude turned out the light. "Think we'll sleep?"

Because we were sharing a bed? His next words said that wasn't what he was concerned about. "Will we have dreams?"

I thought about it. "If I have dreams and start tossing in my sleep, wake me, please."

"Same here."

And somehow, we fell asleep and I hoped I'd not dream, that Jude's presence on the other side of that huge bed would provide a semblance of security that would let me sleep well and long.

No such luck. I did dream. But it was different from any of my dreams so far. Instead of the lake, I dreamed of a road. Just a road. Not the black-topped freeway we'd driven that day, rather it was a narrow gravel road beneath old-growth trees that met overhead, giving travelers a cool, shaded path.

The trees were the same trees of the forest of my dreams and my dream self was eager to see where the road led but the dream ended before I found out. The rest of the night was peaceful and I awoke the next morning rested and refreshed for the first time since the dreams had entered my life. So perhaps Jude's presence had helped after all. Or perhaps it was because we were obeying the compulsion instead of fighting it. Or because the road was rural and cool.

We had breakfast in that restaurant attached to the motel. The compulsion let us eat. We were relieved. At least whatever was behind the compulsion understood that we'd not end up where it wanted us if we couldn't stay alive and evidently eating was necessary, as were normal, human activities like sleeping. And it let us shop for sandwich stuff that we tossed in the back of Jude's SUV on top of our luggage.

But as we did those things we wondered about the entity behind the compulsion, one we couldn't imagine and couldn't picture because we had no idea what kind of person would do such a thing. *Could* do such a thing.

What kind of power did that person have? Was he a magician? A psychic? Or what?

CHAPTER 5

In Jude's SUV, we traveled steadily. We didn't speak because what was there to say? We took turns driving, getting lunch at a locally owned drive-through in some small town whose name we didn't know because we'd not paid attention when we passed the town limits sign in what was becoming a given in our journey. To know nothing and care nothing of our whereabouts beyond the direction we were heading. North, of course. Always north.

We were glad to eat at the fast-food place so as not to have to sit down in a restaurant or make sandwiches for lunch so we could save the makings for some other time. We ate our fast food as Jude drove. I shoved my burger and fries down my throat and crumpled the paper wrappings into a ball to be discarded when we found a dumpster in still another small, unnamed town.

Then I forced myself to inspect the scenery beyond the window though I cared not what it was like. It was rural, that much I noticed and that mattered because the scenery in our dreams was rural. Not exactly like what lay beyond the windows, but similar in that there were few people or houses.

As the hours passed, I watched that scenery change

as we continued north, noting how there were fewer and fewer towns and those we did encounter became successively smaller than the ones we'd already passed through.

I forced myself to notice as the small groves of trees, mostly evergreens, became more plentiful and the farms fewer, with ever larger groves separating one farm from another and those occasional remaining farms becoming smaller and smaller as the groves turned into forest and the farms became subsistence farms instead of large commercial ones until they ceased altogether and we were in the heart of the north woods.

As early afternoon became late afternoon and the sun slid imperceptibly towards the west, the weather changed. I didn't notice until the first few clouds appeared, not enough to hide the sun or dim the bright day, they were mere dots on the western horizon and I didn't know why I noticed them but I did. Perhaps because I was focused on our surroundings in order to prove I was normal and the sky was part of that normal world.

The clouds grew in size though they were still not a concern and turned darker as they moved eastwards across the sky. Towards us. I turned to Jude. "We're in for some rain."

Jude checked the clouds and frowned. "Could be bad." Did pilots know about clouds? "We should start looking for a motel."

"Can we stop? Will the compulsion allow it?"

"I hope so." Because he, too, couldn't be sure what the compulsion would let us do. The whole thing was still new to us. "We might not have a choice if those clouds hold the amount of rain I think they do. Watch for a motel. Anyone will do."

Except there were no motels because the several towns we went through were too small to have more than a general store and gas station. Jude's brow wrinkled into fine lines where there'd been none moments earlier. "Surely there'll be a larger town pretty soon. One with a motel."

"We don't have a map." Maps had seemed irrelevant. We were following a compulsion, not a map.

"Cell phone map?"

So, I checked the map feature of my phone and noted the dot that showed our location and then looked to see what lay ahead. I breathed a sigh of relief. "There's a largish town two hours ahead. Maybe three."

He checked the clouds again. "They're coming fast. We're going to get wet."

"That'll be the worst of it? We'll just get wet?"

"I think so." He examined the road ahead. "It's pavement, not gravel, so it won't turn into mud." He shrugged. "And the traffic is light. If anyone with any sense is watching the weather they'll be off the roads before the storm hits so we'll have the highway to ourselves."

His words were comforting though the clouds, still growing and turning darker as I watched, weren't threatening. No rotation, no building into thick shelf clouds that would push through the sky like a snowplow, bringing devastation. They were just clouds. I leaned back and closed my eyes and tried to sleep.

I couldn't, of course, the compulsion wouldn't allow it, never had so far during our journey, but I willed my body to relax enough that I got some rest, if not actual sleep.

I opened my eyes now and then to covertly inspect the approaching weather as well as the man next to me because, even with the compulsion, I could feel something beyond just the fact of having to go north. I could feel Jude's presence beside me.

I wondered what the feeling was. Took it apart and examined it. And, with chagrin, recognized it for what it was. The man-woman thing. The same attraction I'd felt at the convention when I'd wished we didn't have to go our separate ways.

Jude was all male. He was also all competency and focus, except when he was relaxing, probably good qualities if you flew jets. I knew those things already, had figured them out as we'd sauntered about the convention, but somehow every time I looked at him now – really looked – they were burned into my consciousness all over again. I liked those qualities, had always considered they would be important when I got serious about some guy in my far distant future.

I wanted to sigh but didn't because he'd notice and I didn't want to have to explain myself. Too embarrassing. I hoped that when we stopped for the night if a room was already reserved for us, it would have two beds. Please.

As for Jude, I couldn't help wondering what he saw when he looked at me. I hadn't a clue. Did he look at me the way I looked at him? In the man-woman way? Did he see me at all? Or was I just a passenger on the way to find whatever was driving us north?

The rain hit with a suddenness that sent the SUV towards the shoulder of the road, forcing Jude to grip the steering wheel hard and fight to keep us from going off entirely. But he kept control and soon we were plowing through a downpour so heavy the wipers couldn't keep up and he had to slow down to stay on the road.

It continued that way for a long time. Hours, perhaps? It was hard to tell because it grew so dark that it could have been late evening. Or it could have just been the rain falling from thick, heavy clouds that hid the sun. It was impossible to know the difference. Then true night settled around us and the world turned so scary dark that the headlights barely pierced enough to show the way ahead.

And still Jude drove. He glanced at me. "How far ahead is that town with the motel?"

I checked the cell phone map again. "Not far. An hour at normal speed. With the rain, I don't know."

He nodded that he understood. "We'll get there when we get there." He tried to be positive. "The only thing that matters is that we will sleep on beds tonight, not in the SUV."

I watched how sure his driving was, how skilled, and thought that must be how he handled the jets he flew for whatever corporation he worked for. He was confident of his ability and that confidence made me unafraid.

After an hour of driving, long enough to have reached that motel in good weather but not now because the driving rain added to that time and I'd accepted that we still had a long way to go, I looked ahead and saw a light ahead in the black of night. Not a town. Not a house. It was another vehicle coming towards us beyond a curve in the highway. The first vehicle since the downpour had started.

It should have been fine. We should have passed that other vehicle, a semi-truck, as we rounded that curve, without incident. Both vehicles were in their proper lanes. Nothing should have gone wrong.

But it did. The semi hit a slippery spot and slid out of control. Jude stepped on the gas and the SUV responded. It leapt ahead and Jude steered towards the side of the road to avoid being run over as the semi swung back and forth as the driver tried to regain control of his huge vehicle. We slid every which way as the semi came closer and still closer to us until inches separated us and I knew we were going to crash.

Jude's hands on the wheel kept the SUV headed away from the semi and put it into an intentional sidewise slide. The SUV slid past the semi, then turned completely around twice before the wheels grabbed the gravel of the shoulder and we straightened out.

Then it was all over and both vehicles continued on their way. Except Jude pulled to a stop on the side of the road, emergency flashers on, and put his head down on the steering wheel and just sat that way for a long time.

I reached for him. Touched him. Put my hand on his and hoped it was the right thing to do and, eventually, he sat up, took a deep breath, turned to look at me though we couldn't truly see each other in the dark, and said, "I almost got us killed."

"No. The semi almost got us killed. You saved us."

"We need to stop. This downpour isn't safe."

"The town isn't far."

He nodded and after a moment he pulled back onto the road and continued on slowly and carefully through that insane downpour. There were no more near-misses because there were no other vehicles on the road and half an hour later the lights of a medium-sized town appeared and we coasted to a stop beneath the canopy of the only motel in town. The one that we were sure had a room waiting for us because so far there'd always been one.

A half hour after that we were eating dinner in the room reserved for us. It was in disposable containers from the restaurant near the motel that was used to travelers wanting something to take back to their rooms.

Would we always eat so during the trip? It seemed so. We finished, tossed our containers in the trash and looked at one another. Jude smiled slightly and quirked one eyebrow. "One room again. One bed."

"In this downpour, I'm glad to be anywhere out of the weather."

"Toss you for choosing which side of the bed you get."

"Heads I choose the side I want, tails you do."

I lost but it didn't matter. Dry sheets and soft pillows were all that mattered and soon we both slept. Not well because the usual dreams intruded, waking us intermittently. Until, as we grew accustomed to the dark and could make out each other's outline and saw each other come awake at the same time, we realized something. "We are not only dreaming the same dream, we are dreaming it at the same time." Because we woke from it at the same time.

A chill went along my spine. "It's worse than I thought. Who is putting the dreams into our minds? And how? What kind of person can force dreams into both of us at the same time? And why?"

Jude's reply was dry. "More efficient that way. One dream, one effort, two recipients."

We weren't sleeping so we sat up, leaning against the headboard though we didn't turn on a light. "Forget the why of the thing. How can anyone do it? What magic do they possess?"

"Some black ops kind of thing?"

"Then why us? We're nobody. A corporate jet pilot and a bookkeeper who raises puppies."

A long silence followed, made more poignant by the darkness that pooled around us, the only light being flashes of lightning seen through a crack in the room darkening drapes because the storm hadn't yet ended.

Jude reached out and took my hand. We each remained on our side of the bed but the warmth of him was welcome. The reassurance of him.

"Whatever is happening is being done with skill. Whomever is doing this knows his business. He's an expert."

"He not only knows how to do it, he knows us. He's learned about us somehow. He's done his homework. Because he's called us by name."

I spoke slowly. "There's only one person who knows us both."

We both said his name at the same time. "Lourdes Jones."

"But he was so sweet. So nice."

"And the iced tea he gave us that last day wasn't the same as the tea we bought later from the same place."

"What was in it?"

I felt Jude's shrug. "Something more powerful than anything I can imagine."

"Black ops doesn't sound so crazy anymore."

"He didn't seem like a man in black to me. Which brings us back to the first question. Why us?"

"You, perhaps, Jude. I can see you being of interest to black ops types. You fly jets."

He laughed. "For CEOs who like dogs." He shook his head. "It's not black ops. It's something else."

"But what?"

After a long pause, Jude said, "We'll find out when we reach the end of our trip."

We eventually slid back beneath the covers and tried to sleep. We failed, of course, and when daylight finally showed, thin and dark because the horrendous storm, though it had lessened, had become an all-day rain. We were as tired as when we'd gone to bed.

"I wish we could get a good night's sleep."

"Lourdes Jones won't let us."

"It might not be him. It could be those black ops guys."

Jude turned to me, eyes dark and deep and weary. "We know nothing for sure."

He was right. Any conclusion would be pure speculation. But we knew a few things. We knew we weren't random subjects. We knew we'd deliberately been chosen by someone who knew us both and since Lourdes Jones was the only person who did, he was the most likely suspect.

CHAPTER 6

We tried to get some more sleep and succeeded a bit. But we had to leave eventually. As I came fully awake, though, I noticed something. The urgency behind the compulsion to travel north was less than it had been the previous morning. I also noticed that the rain was letting up, gradually being replaced by a timid sun that promised to do its best to come out as soon as the last clouds rolled past.

I wondered if the two were related. If the entity behind the compulsion knew about the rain and was allowing for it. Or if it knew how close we'd come to having an accident and was concerned that we might not make it north.

The lessening of the overwhelming urgency to go north was luxurious. My teeth no longer ached from clenching them. I could stretch sinuously in that huge bed and brush my teeth later in the bathroom without almost being overcome by angst. I could think about what to wear. And I could do all of those things even though they took minutes away from travel.

Were we being given the gift of extra time because we'd been obedient and were doing what the entity wanted? Or was it because we were heading north and just going in the right direction had a positive effect on us? Or, more likely, was it because we'd almost died during the storm and it wouldn't have use for us if we were dead so whomever was behind our trip decided to give us a respite to recover from our ordeal?

Whatever the reason, as we headed for breakfast, we were grateful to dawdle over a meal and enjoy it. To notice what we were eating. To be human.

When we finished, rose, and headed outside, we took full advantage of the release from the need to immediately go north. We bought an umbrella in a store in the middle of town and walked to a nearby bridge and watched white-water rafters laugh in what was by then a light rain as they plunged through a foamy river and we held our hands out to feel the droplets.

We luxuriated in the wet day and strolled about much as we'd done at the convention, except this time we admired white-water rafters instead of service dogs and spoke of how mysterious and beautiful the day was, viewed as it was through a curtain of misty rain and part of the beauty was that we were free enough of the compulsion to actually notice it.

By mid-afternoon, though, it was clear the reprieve had been temporary because the compulsion returned. Suddenly. Between one step and the next as we explored the river and the town along its banks. It wasn't as strong as at first but we couldn't ignore it. We tried but all that happened was that we both soon broke out in a sweat and began trembling. Even Jude, the ultimate tough guy couldn't control his body. So, we soon found our steps heading towards his SUV.

And we drove north once more.

Always north.

We didn't have lunch before leaving those white-water rafters because the compulsion hit so hard and suddenly that we had to get going. North, of course. "Guess we should be grateful we had breakfast." Jude's eyes rolled as we climbed into his SUV.

We should have grabbed snacks because as Jude drove my stomach rumbled with hunger. By that time, we'd passed out of rural areas and into thick forest with long stretches of road without houses, stores, gas stations or any place to eat.

Of course, if there had been those things, we'd not have stopped long enough to have a real meal anyway. The compulsion wouldn't have allowed it. It was as if it was making up for the time we'd lost while we were being allowed to relax. So, we were glad we still had the makings of sandwiches in a cooler.

When the middle of the day came Jude coasted to the side of the road and then onto a secondary road that meandered through a clearing in the forest. He slowed to a stop and stared through the steering wheel at a normal scene. I was sure he was thinking the same thing I was. That nothing was normal about our current situation.

After a brief respite for sandwiches seated in his SUV while wondering if the compulsion would ever let us stop for decent meals after this or if we'd have to subsist forever on sandwiches made in motel rooms and eaten on the fly, we resumed our trip. North, always north, but that day we covered less than half the distance of the previous days due to our late start but also possibly because by then we were on narrow country roads.

After we registered at still another motel, also with

a room waiting for us, and I'd slid into still another huge bed after a decent though hurried meal in the restaurant connected to the motel, I felt almost human. I somehow managed to get a good night's sleep, waking with time to clean up so I could follow Jude to the motel restaurant. He'd gone ahead and ordered for both of us because by then we knew what each of us liked to eat as well as what position we preferred sleeping in. As if we were an old married couple.

That morning, getting ready for the day, as I stared at myself in the mirror, I saw something different. I saw me without circles beneath my eyes. I thought about it. I'd had a restful night. How? As I stared at that mirror, I realized something. I'd had no dreams. None.

Why not? I reached deep into myself and searched for the compulsion to see if it had lessened still more. What I found inside of myself stunned me.

The compulsion was still there but I could act like a normal human being. It had changed. It had come to know me and what I needed in order to function. And it allowed for that.

I ran out of the motel room to tell Jude. I found him waiting for me outside the restaurant, hands in his pockets. When I approached him, he took one look at me and said, "It's let up for you too. Hasn't it?"

We just stood there and stared at each other, uncertain what to do. What to say. How to feel. Jude touched me. Just touched me as if to see if I was real because what had just happened was so momentous that neither of us could process it. "We can be normal." His voice was full of wonderment. "Somewhat normal. We still must go north but we can be human beings during the trip."

We stared at each other barely aware that we were standing in front of the restaurant door like a couple of idiots until Jude held out his hand to me and we went inside and it felt odd walking beside him like a normal couple.

It felt more than odd. It felt right, as it had felt at the convention but then we'd thought nothing of it. Now Jude turned to me and took my hand as he'd done at the convention and that simple act was proof we were once again the people we'd been back then. At least we were close to being those people. Close to being normal again.

A warmth spread through me even as I wished in some remote corner of my mind that the handholding was more than the simple release from a compulsion that had held us for what had seemed like forever.

Had Jude ever thought of me as I thought of him? Way back at the convention, perhaps? Had he thought me attractive? He'd seemed as reluctant to part from me that last day of the convention as I'd been to part from him. But did he remember that feeling we'd shared and would he want to resurrect it now that we could think for ourselves? Was he seeing me in that man-woman way? The answer to that question was important and I knew I'd not dare ask it out loud.

Instead, we discussed the let-up of the compulsion rationally as if we were discussing the time of day over a breakfast that we actually enjoyed. Eggs over easy, bacon, and toast, with a side order of orange juice. Jude had two eggs to my one but otherwise they were the same. We raised our glasses to each other and clinked them in a toast to our new freedom exactly as we'd clinked glasses of iced tea at the convention.

We lingered over breakfast far longer than we should have done because the luxury of not having to get on the road to head north immediately was so amazing as to be decadent, and when we finished, we packed in a leisurely manner and checked out as if we had all the time in the world.

Because we did. Though the compulsion thrummed in us in a way we couldn't ignore, we also, in a way, felt like we had forever.

We didn't head north again immediately and the compulsion was like a voice in the back of our heads telling us we could take a break so long as it wasn't too long. We looked at each other like conspirators and chose to explore the lovely, quaint town we were in that we'd not noticed when we arrived because the compulsion had driven everything else from our minds. The rain had ended and the sun was bright and warm and we meandered through shops and along a groomed trail that wound through the nearby forest where people walked and occasional runners got their daily exercise.

We held hands and as time passed I knew that it was intentional on Jude's part and not a part of the compulsion and that knowledge sent something in me soaring, though at first I told myself it could merely be because we'd shared the same unsettling experience and if he felt a need to be close to someone who knew what it was like, well I was the only person who could make that claim.

Except it might be more than that. I hoped it was. I'd been attracted to Jude from the very beginning. The bulk of him. His solid body. The way he hovered protectively without seeming to realize what he was doing that he did simply because he was that kind of man. The question was, was he similarly be attracted to me?

Was it possible? Now that the compulsion was letting us once again think and feel like human beings, could the man-woman thing take up where it had ended when we left the convention? Could something serious grow between us?

If so, did I want it?

Absolutely! The knowledge jarred me and I almost stopped dead still when the knowledge hit me how deeply attracted to Jude I was. Love? Maybe. Maybe not. But attraction? Most assuredly!

We walked for hours along that trail, speaking now and then, mostly luxuriating quietly in the freedom of not having to go north at once. We had lunch and then later, dinner, in that same motel restaurant and each time we lingered over our meal we learned more and more about each other because, wonder of wonders, we could think about everyday things. And about each other.

He had three sisters and a brother and had wanted to fly planes since childhood, so had joined the Air Force and stayed in it until he wanted a different life and had become a corporate jet pilot. But he wasn't done yet, he said, he'd not found his final niche. He didn't know what the next phase of his life might be other than it would have to do with flying in some way or other.

My story was similar. I was a good accountant with a decent customer base and could continue on that way forever but I'd become restless lately and decided I needed to find another direction for my life though I didn't know what direction that would be.

"Did he know that about us? The man behind the compulsion? Did he sense we were at a crossroads and did that fact somehow enter into his decision to do this to us?"

We didn't know if our restlessness had been obvious in that convention even as we knew we should be happy with what we already had because, if nothing else, the compulsion had taught us to appreciate everyday things. We finally, in embarrassment, agreed that we were still looking. Searching. And would continue to do so until we found what we sought, whether the entity behind the compulsion knew about it or not.

We stayed up late that night, watching the stars from a bench in front of the motel. We didn't talk, we just sat and took in the night and the world around us. When we finally headed for bed, I thought Jude was going to kiss me. Or do something romantic. But he didn't.

So much for wishful thinking.

"Have a good night's sleep," he said instead, knowing how important sleep was, something we'd learned only when dreams had taken it from us.

"You too," I managed, struggling to hide my disappointment as I crawled into my side of the bed, acknowledging that anything romantic while we shared a bed was probably not a good idea.

I began the night sleeping soundly. No dreams, no tossing and turning, nothing out of the ordinary. But then, subtly at first, then a bit stronger until, in one huge wallop that sent me into a sitting position in one stunned move, the compulsion returned full force.

We'd had enough of a vacation. Now all I could

think of was direction. North. I had to go north. The urge was so strong I got out of bed and headed for my suitcase so I could dress and continue my journey in the middle of the night. Because something was waiting for me when I reached my destination and I had to find it. Needed to. The compulsion made me want whatever waited for me.

I almost packed and left but I stopped because I was with Jude. I had no vehicle and didn't have the keys to his SUV. I couldn't go anywhere. But I found myself pacing across the small motel room floor. I opened the room darkening drapes and stared at the night sky, blazing with stars and a new moon and those things and everything else in my surroundings, the curtains, the very walls, were all telling me to go north.

And I waited for Jude to wake up because he was feeling the same compulsion I was and knew that soon he'd be beside me and he'd need to go north too. Just as I did.

CHAPTER 7

Jude was slower to come awake than I was but it happened as I knew it would. He crawled out of bed and staggered toward me and we simply stared at one another until he sank back onto the side of the bed, putting his head in his hands. "It's back".

I'd been up longer than he had, though, so I knew something he hadn't noticed. "It's back but it's different. Changed."

He thought and seemed to be listening, sensing, reading what was happening in his mind to figure it out. He soon nodded that he, too, also noticed the difference. "It's not just a need to go north anymore. There's more. There's now something behind the compulsion. A mind. Thoughts."

"A person."

"Is someone talking to us? Mentally?"

"I think so. He wants us to know why we should go north and he's going to tell us something."

"No!" Jude touched me. Pulled me close. Made me look at him as he said, "Don't listen. Whoever is behind this is trying to pull us deeper into its web. We must fight it. We mustn't believe any of it no matter what it says."

I shivered. Jude wrapped his arms tight around me and we sat for a long time. Then he moved, pulling me closer as if doing so could make us both safe but I was afraid and he felt my fear.

"It'll be okay." I burrowed into him because he was trying to protect me and I didn't care that he couldn't change things, that he couldn't protect us from the compulsion. The knowledge that he wanted to sent warmth through me. And hope.

Then he spoke. "Way back when it first started, you said we should fight it." His arms held me still tighter. "You were right. It's what we should have done."

His hands roamed over my back as I moved enough within his embrace to look straight at him. Eyeball to eyeball. "No, Jude, I was wrong. You were right. We must confront it. We have to. It's the only way." He'd been right way back then and I had to make him know that now. "If we are to live normally again, we must find the source. See it. Talk to it. Because it'll never leave us alone."

"We don't know that for sure."

"We don't know any other possibility."

He gathered me close. Then, as suddenly as a light turning on, he grinned. I could feel the laughter in his chest build as he accepted what I'd said and he continued to hold me tight and then tighter still. "Okay. We'll continue north. We'll confront it but it'll be more than a confrontation. When we reach the end of this hellish journey you're going to hear me yell. Loudly. And you'll probably hear words you've never heard before and shouldn't ever hear."

I smiled along with him, glorying in the feel of him

and in his grin because with his arms wrapped around me I felt invincible and whatever we chose to do would be right because we'd be doing it together. So I laughed. Then I said, "I'll back you up. Just tell me what to say. Teach me a few wonderful words. I'll scream."

Our smiles faded but we remained so close that for all intents and purposes our bodies were one. Jude's arm grew tighter around me and I made no attempt to move away because he was warm and exactly what I wanted and I greedily drew his warmth into me. He was what I needed. Someone solid. And sensible.

Most of all, he was unafraid. He was a safe harbor in the storm that my life had become and when had that pure male something about him become multiplied so many times that it now radiated from his every pore and turned me into something that couldn't resist him and couldn't live without him?

Our eyes met and slid away. I didn't want him to read me because his body next to mine was doing things to me that I couldn't hide from him. Things I'd wished for at the convention that hadn't happened because we went our separate ways. Those feelings had returned in force and were growing exponentially.

I spoke into his chest. "So, in spite of the change, in spite of everything that's happened, we are still going north."

"Yep. I was momentarily weak but you got me past it. We must confront whatever is doing this to us." Eventually he unwrapped me, rose, and headed for the door. "So, we continue north and when we find the source we'll do something. I don't know what but we'll get our lives back and that's a promise."

He paused at the door. I smiled wanly, sucking whatever residual warmth I could get from across the room into me as I said one word. "North."

He opened the door. Stopped and closed it again without going outside. Came back to me. Looked at me experimentally and leaned down and kissed me long and hard. Our arms went around each other and we rocked together and kissed still more. When we came apart neither of us said anything because what was there to say?

Then we heard it. The voice from that first day that wasn't quite normal without knowing in what way it wasn't. A voice in our minds that we both recognized. "I'm afraid you have no choice because I need you. So you will go north." The voice paused. "But the trip north is just the first stage of your journey."

Jude stared at nothing until he asked loudly, "There's more when we reach wherever we are going?"

The voice spoke again, placatingly. "A new and exciting life is waiting for you at the end of your journey. A life of adventure."

Jude and I looked at each other. "What do you mean? What kind of life?"

"You'll find out. Your love for each other will not be interfered with because love is important. I know. I did my research." And that was all. The voice ended and we were left staring at each other. Neither of us mentioned the specifics. Adventure. Love. Neither of us. It would be too embarrassing.

When we put our packed bags in the back of Jude's SUV as we'd done every other morning, we enjoyed another leisurely breakfast. The compulsion was back but we were reclaiming our humanity and knew we could do some everyday things. We could be human.

Jude tipped his chair back on two legs, something I was sure the restaurant manager wouldn't approve of but that proved he could be normal and do normal things. "I might just sit here when we are done eating and drink coffee until it's time for lunch."

I examined the menu without hurrying and ordered what I wanted instead of the first thing I saw and Jude did the same and it was pure bliss because the compulsion didn't force us to hurry. Until the waitresses' scowl said we were lingering too long and she had other customers to take care of.

So, we chose our food and enjoyed watching the waitress move to other customers, skirt swishing in irritation. Our looks met in a joint smile because we'd actually noticed another human being going about their daily life. Even her poorly hidden anger was wonderful.

And then the compulsion hit once more. Hard. As if it knew what we were doing and was reasserting its dominance and making sure we knew it had authority over us after all.

It worked. There was no way we could ignore it even though we put our minds together and pushed back against it.

But our effort had one result. The entity entered our minds once more and it communicated again even as our teeth gnashed because we were sick and tired of it. And we were stunned by what it said.

It apologized for pushing us so hard.

Jude's chair slowly, carefully, came back so all four legs were on the floor as we both heard it. It spoke directly to our minds but the words were clear and unmistakable as everyone else in the café went about their business because they couldn't hear a word.

It wanted us to know it was sorry. It hadn't realized how vulnerable we were. How fragile. It wasn't used to dealing with fragile beings. With humans. To date it had only dealt with sturdier species. It hadn't meant to frighten us. It promised to be more considerate in the future.

The entity continued. It made sure we understood that, though it would be more considerate of our fragility in the future, it was still important that we go north. That we complete our journey. That we finish our mission because we were needed and it had not had the foresight to choose anyone other than the two of us so we must finish what we started. Us. Jude and me. Because we were the only ones. We were the 'two.'

It was confident it had done well in choosing us. It was absolutely sure we were right for the job. It knew our pair bond was solid and that it would become strong and still stronger as time passed. Because it had met us and studied us.

It explained how it had studied humans in general for quite a while and us specifically and had learned about pair bonding and so knew what it was talking about. It had learned humans needed the companionship of other humans and had ascertained that the kind of companionship between a man and woman who were matched both for emotional and intellectual compatibility was preferred. It said it believed the proper term for that human quality was 'love.'

"Love?" Jude said it out loud as our looks met in stunned amazement and loud enough that people at nearby tables looked our way. "It thinks we're in love?"

The entity continued with its explanation. It was

sure we'd be delighted with what waited for us at the end of our journey. It was glad we were such a wonderful couple. It was sure we'd live happily ever after. Like happened in books.

Jude and I stared at each other across the table. "We're supposed to be in love?"

"Like in books? Like in fiction?"

"It thinks we already are."

My thoughts went back to the service dog convention. I remembered the courtly, old-fashioned man I'd found so fascinating. So different. So unusual. "Lourdes Jones played matchmaker at the convention."

"And we went along with it."

Jude examined me across the table. "Lourdes must be behind the compulsion."

"Or some other unknown entity was at the convention and was watching? It saw Lourdes Jones playing matchmaker and thought we were in love."

"That makes more sense. It as much as admitted it isn't human. But Lourdes is."

"It might not know men and women can act like they are in love without it being real."

"It might think a simple kiss is the same as a life-long attachment."

"It thought that our holding hands at the convention meant we were in love."

We stared at each other across the table. "So we now know how and why we were chosen. We know where it found us. What we don't know is what it wants from us. Or who it is. *What* it is because it clearly isn't human."

We finished eating. Jude rose, came to my side of the table, and pulled me up beside him. "Let's get going and meet the SOB at the end of this journey."

I let him lead me into the bright sunshine. He held my hand, looked about, and dared the entity to interpret the very human act of holding hands in whatever way it chose. Romantic, if it was watching and it probably was. Evidence of pair bonding.

We headed for his SUV, climbed in and started north once more.

Before we'd gone a block, the engine died.

CHAPTER 8

We coasted to the side of the road. "Now what?" Jude rolled his eyes and sighed. "Don't we have enough problems without a vehicle that won't go anywhere?" He got out and looked under the hood and gave another sigh. "We need a tow truck."

The good news was we didn't have to be towed very far because we were still in town. The bad news was they didn't have the belt the SUV needed and couldn't get it until the

next day. "Sorry, but that's the way it is." The mechanic looked us up and down. Something about us told him we weren't local. "There's a motel in town. Maybe they have a vacancy."

"The same motel we stayed at last night."

"The only one in town."

Jude was fatalistic. "Maybe we'll get the same room."

The mechanic hung the SUV keys on a rack alongside a dozen or so other sets of keys for various vehicles to be repaired. "Better hurry. It fills up fast."

"In a smallish out-of-the-way town in the middle of nowhere?"

"Depends on the weather." The mechanic rolled his

eyes. "It rained yesterday. It poured. No one with any common sense came to town then." He scanned the cloudless sky. "Today's different. It's a great day to get outside. Go somewhere. Do something. On days like this, tourists come to town by the hundreds."

He considered the forest closing in around the town and the specialty shops along the town's single street that were there only because enough tourists arrived on good days to keep them in business. He was clearly proud of his home. "Town will be busy today. So the motel will fill up fast."

We walked the short distance to the motel and discovered the mechanic was right. "One room left and you're lucky to get it." Jude used his credit card for the first time since starting our trip for a room that wasn't already booked in our names because the entity behind the compulsion couldn't have known we'd have car trouble.

The room wouldn't be ready for several hours so we left our suitcases in Jude's SUV and took a tour of the town because it was something to do. It was difficult with the compulsion pressuring us to go north even though we didn't have a vehicle but we struggled through it. As the hours passed the compulsion grew increasingly difficult to ignore. I was sweating. Jude was so antsy he could barely walk straight.

"So much for the entity's consideration of our fragile human selves. This is torture."

The tension grew worse as the hours passed. When lunchtime neared, we knew we'd not be able to sit in a restaurant. Too antsy.

we bought the fixings for a picnic along with a tarp to lay on the ground and found a spot on the side of the highway on a hill with a view of the surrounding terrain that was lovely and far enough from the road itself that neither the sounds nor the rush of traffic reached us. A place we could relax. If the compulsion would allow it. Or where we could pace. Or jump up and down. Or simply go crazy.

We made sandwiches and opened cans of pop and pretended we were enjoying a picnic. We told ourselves we were dealing with the compulsion just fine. We pretended to relax. But we couldn't because we couldn't sit still. We could barely eat for the tension in our bodies. We fairly thrummed with the stress.

When we'd managed to eat enough to ward off starvation, we tried earnestly to relax. We lay on the tarp and stared at the sky and told each other it was a beautiful day. Jude was the first to give up. He groaned while staring unseeing at the trees above us. "It's bad. Really bad."

I unhappily agreed. "And getting worse." Which it was, minute by agonizing minute.

I turned on my side to see him better. Sunlight filtered through the trees and turned him into a thing of light and shadows as that flickering sunlight moved across his body in rhythm with the slight wind that sent the few clouds that remained from the recent storm scudding across the sky.

Then I rolled onto my back once again because watching him was way too erotic. Instead, I watched those clouds, so white and clean and innocent, as I couldn't avoid the effect Jude on the tarp had on me, his body filled with tension and his mind with frustration.

I wished it was just the two of us on that tarp beneath that blue sky and that we were having a real picnic. I wished the compulsion wasn't a third party to our day and that it would let us have this time to ourselves since we couldn't continue our journey.

I thought about our situation. Then I thought some more. Then I grew truly angry at the entity behind the compulsion and the more I thought, the angrier I grew. "It's not fair." I didn't try to hide my frustration. "The entity can talk to us and it does so whenever it has something to say. Why can't we talk to it and tell it we're having car trouble and that it should leave us alone?"

The frustration was getting to Jude too, though, to be honest, he wasn't a placid individual in the best of times. If I was bad, he was worse. He was a pilot. He was used to doing things. He needed action. Now he punched the ground beside him but all the good it did was to get him some skinned knuckles. "Good idea and just how do you suggest we talk to something that doesn't exist? Do we scream into thin air and hope it hears?"

"Sorry. I was just venting. I have no idea how to contact the entity or even if it's possible."

Jude took another bite of the sandwich he'd been ignoring, chomping down with an irritated growl, licking his fingers and then inspecting them for crumbs. The simple gesture curled my insides. But as he'd been eating, he'd also been thinking. "The entity speaks to our minds. Maybe we should talk to it the same way it talks to us. Maybe it'll hear."

"And how do you propose we do that? We can't read minds let alone talk to them."

Neither of us came up with any specific idea but he was on to something. Maybe we should try talking to the entity mind to mind. So thinking, I did what I supposed mind readers did. I squeezed my eyes shut and mentally told an entity I couldn't visualize or begin to understand that we needed a break. I mentally enunciated each word carefully and slowly. Then I repeated myself.

It didn't work. I heard nothing back and the compulsion didn't ease up. I told Jude what I'd done and that it hadn't worked. He tried it, shrugging to say anything was worth a try and then doing pretty much the same thing I did but with no better success.

"That idea was a dud." His frustration grew in tandem with the compulsion that was growing exponentially as we lay there and didn't go north. Soon I'd be screaming in pain.

Hoping he wouldn't take it the wrong way while also hoping he would take it exactly how I wished, I reached for him. I needed some of his male toughness to help lessen the stress that was growing ever stronger and making me so restless I could barely tolerate lying still on that tarp. The stress of the entity was increasing because we weren't obedient and weren't heading north.

Jude almost absent mindedly put out an arm for me to use as a pillow. Thankful for the gesture I lay on his arm, enjoying the scent of man and pine needles, glad for the emotional closeness because it blocked at least some of the power of the compulsion. And because I liked the feel of him.

But it was more than that. The compulsion had been slightly blocked when Jude and I came together. It had let up and, as I thought about it, I knew it had to be because I was close to Jude, both physically and emotionally and was borrowing his emotional strength.

I thought about it still more. I concentrated on his arm supporting me instead of on the compulsion. I felt the scent of pine and man that warmed my middle and I thought about them with every fiber of my being instead of thinking about going north. Just north.

I wasn't the only one who noticed that slight but very real difference. Jude noticed it too. The lessening of stress as we lay together. "Together we can hold it at bay. Somehow." I heard his husky words, the sound of him, the deep timbre that sent shock waves through me. "It's the two of us together. The closeness of us. It's blocking the compulsion. It's just a bit but it's something."

"So?"

He reached for the sky with his free hand. Waved it in the fresh, scented air. "Think about it. We can ignore the compulsion if we are focusing on us instead of on it. I know you feel the change because I feel it and we always feel the entity the same way."

He wrapped me closer to his body. "The entity doesn't know we had car trouble. If it did, it would probably ease up because it said it cares about us. Maybe it does. We think it does. But it's not the entity that's causing that momentary easing of tension. It's us. We are doing it. Us. You and me. Together."

"But how?"

He rolled until he was facing me. Then his arm beneath my head moved and he used both of his arms to reach for me. He deliberately rolled me onto my side until I was fully facing him. Then he moved closer and still closer until we were mere inches apart. Then he pulled me even closer until our bodies fit so tightly together that a piece of paper couldn't fit between us.

Then he kissed me, as he'd done before but somehow this time was different. Intentional. He slowly wrapped me in his arms while rolling on top of me. He held me tighter and still tighter. And he kissed me again. Harder. Thoroughly. Completely. Until I was not only breathless but was kissing him back with everything in me.

Then he pulled back just enough to look at me and whisper very, very quietly. "It's gone."

It took me a moment to figure out what he was referring to because my body was on fire. Then I got it. "The compulsion. It's gone."

"Because we made an emotional connection when we came together and that connection made the compulsion disappear."

"The two of us kissing?" The idea was so preposterous I should have laughed. But I didn't because the compulsion was truly gone.

His look begged me to understand. "It's the pure, unadulterated emotion of us coming together. Of us being joined. Passion is an elemental emotion and evidently it overrides everything else including the compulsion."

"So we should have sex?"

His eyes sparked and his whole demeanor changed. He was a warrior seeing victory. "Maybe we don't have to go that far but now we know the compulsion is emotional in nature so a competing emotion, one that's stronger, can drown it out."

I luxuriated in the feel of the man with me and the lack of the compulsion to go north while realizing at some level how impractical sex would be as a deterrent.

"Why'd we not figure this out sooner?"

"Because we've been circumspect. So far." He was exultant.

I giggled. I couldn't help it. Though my body was on fire his thoughts weren't practical. Not at all. "Unfortunately we can't spend every minute of every day in each other's arms."

His answer was in his chuckle. "Unfortunately, nice as we feel together we do need time for eating, sleeping, working, and everything else people do in their daily lives. So maybe my suggestion isn't exactly actionable."

"And it won't get us home."

He grinned and, so close to him, I felt his smile more than saw it. "So for now what we just learned is an intellectually interesting idea but not immediately useful." His grin turned wicked. "But you never know when it might prove to be an asset."

With which we moved even closer together if such was possible and tried every known method of kissing and a few we made up as Jude's hands roved over my backside and mine along his chest and I didn't know it we were doing it to forestall the compulsion or because it felt good.

But nothing lasts forever and the time came when we had to break apart and sit up. People have to breathe. They have to move. They have to exist. They can't kiss forever. So we rose until we stood and stared at one another and embarrassment hit. Hard. I felt my face grow red and Jude didn't meet my look.

And the compulsion returned.

Accepting the reality of the situation, Jude heaved a huge sigh, took my face in one hand and forced us to look at each other even though we didn't want to see in each other's eyes what we'd just been doing. "Let's accept that it's weird. This whole situation is weird." He sighed.

I sighed along with him. "I just wish we could talk to the darned entity behind the compulsion."

"We will. Somehow." His face turned red and his shoulders hunched. "But sex will have to wait."

With which we gathered our picnic things and looked towards town and the motel where we'd spend the night.

CHAPTER 9

As we checked the ground to be sure we'd not left any trash, something occurred to me that we should have thought about earlier and hadn't. "When we tried to communicate with the entity, we spoke mentally. We didn't talk out loud."

Jude stopped in the middle of folding the tarp. "Should we have?" It had spoken to us mentally.

"It knows a lot about us. It's scary how much it knows. But it only knows what we said out loud. If it could read our minds, it would know we're not in love. So it must only know what it hears us say out loud."

We put the picnic leftovers in a paper bag to drop later in a dumpster. As Jude thought over what I'd said, he dropped the bag to the ground, gave me a look that said anything was worth a try. "But it does hear us speak. Like in the convention when I overheard us with Lourdes Jones." Then he took a deep breath, and shouted.

"Hey! Entity! We can't go anywhere today. My car broke down." He paused to listen a moment. When we heard nothing, he then finished with, "So why don't you give us a break? Let up on the pressure until the car is fixed."

I added my own little speech, feeling foolish talking to thin air, but I did it. "We'll get there eventually, whomever you are. We'll still go north. We promise. Really. It'll take a bit longer because of the car repairs but we're coming."

As soon as our words were spoken, we heard a reply in our minds. "Of course you must wait for your vehicle to be repaired." Then, as if it had taken a moment to think things over, it added, "But I will continue with occasional reminders so you don't forget to come when the repairs are complete."

We could communicate with the entity. We could talk to it. In the future we'd take full advantage of that fact. For now, though, Jude had a few things to say and he was so angry that he didn't hold back. "A reminder? Is that what you call this compulsion that's driving us nuts? That's kept us from sleeping or doing just about anything at all until just recently and then you only let up a tiny bit? Just a tiny bit."

He warmed up to his subject. "We know you have an agenda. We get it. But maybe you should remember that we're human. We can only take so much and you're close to pushing us over the edge and that won't get you what you want." He put his hands in his pockets and spread his legs apart in a defiant stance as he stuck his head forward and shouted to the sky. "Understand?!"

The voice in our minds turned placating. Soothing. "Yes, I do understand. Truly. And I regret coming on so hard before I realized how fragile you are."

The entity continued. "But I also know that humans need to be reminded now and then. I don't know why, but they do. They are forgetful beings. They are unique in that respect though it doesn't mean they lack intellect. It's just the way they are made." We heard puzzlement in the mental speech. It didn't understand us. It truly didn't.

Well, we didn't understand it either.

The entity went silent for a moment before continuing. "The things is, I need you, both of you, and time is running out. I believe you are the right people for the job. I know you are. I did extensive research and you two came out the clear winners." We could almost hear it sigh. "If you promise you'll come as soon as possible and won't forget, I'll not remind you quite as often as previously. Or as strongly."

There was another pause, then, "But I will remind you occasionally because it's important that you come so you can see what I'm proposing and make your decision."

Decision? What decision? Jude and I looked at each other but said nothing. What the entity had just told us was huge. We were going to be allowed to make a decision. It hadn't mentioned such a possibility before.

Following another pause, it said more. "I'll relent as long as you continue coming north, that is. If you turn around, I'm afraid I'll have to return to my former somewhat more strident tactics. The ones I shouldn't have used and wouldn't have if I'd known humans to be such fragile beings."

Regret was in its next words. "I see now that I should have recruited more humans in case not all of them worked out or were willing. More than two, anyway. I didn't feel it necessary at the time but it might have made things easier if there were alternates.

But there aren't."

Jude squeezed my hand so hard the circulation was cut because having a conversation with something that wasn't there, couldn't be seen or heard, and wasn't human was truly strange. He pulled me close and whispered so it wouldn't hear us. "We're talking to something that doesn't exist. And it's replying."

"It wants our cooperation."

"Which means it needs us."

He bent closer, touching his lips to my ear, sending shock waves through me caused both by his words and the feel of him. "We can hope things work out but don't be fooled by its nice speech. Don't believe anything it says, good or bad. Like how it said we have a choice. Maybe we do. But don't count on it."

The following night was difficult. In fact, difficult didn't begin to describe it. We knew the best way to get a good night's sleep was to curl together and let the natural feelings such closeness invited take over until the heated emotion that closeness created would send the compulsion away.

Problem was that very emotion made the sleep that we both craved an impossibility. I wanted Jude and he wanted me and neither of us would admit it or do anything about it so we were uncomfortable the entire night but dared not separate because we couldn't count on the compulsion staying away.

It was a very strange night.

When morning arrived, we were so embarrassed we could barely speak to each other or move about the motel room without bumping into each other, followed each time by an apology, with each apology followed by our jumping apart, doing something else and then bumping into each other all over again. Our faces were red every time it happened.

I finally had enough. I grabbed Jude's shirt and pushed him towards the bathroom. "You first and if you say a single word about yesterday or last night, I'll scream."

He tried and failed to get away from me because I had a fistful of his tee shirt. He finally gave in and turned towards the bathroom. But before he entered, though, as he grabbed his suitcase containing a change of clothes, he gave me a murderous look. "I have no intention of saying anything because what is there to say? I just spent the weirdest night of my life sleeping in the most ridiculous positions possible for the strangest reason ever, wanting to do something about it while knowing that would be the worst thing to do because we are, after all, still semi-strangers but mostly because that's what the entity wants and I'm not about to let it win."

He glowered at the wall as if it was the enemy. "So what is there to say? Nothing. Absolutely nothing." With which he stomped into the bathroom, slammed the door and emerged half an hour later looking reasonably human.

I took my turn and could have stayed in the shower forever, letting the hot water run over my body without thinking because he was right and I was glad we'd done nothing about our feelings. But if we'd have let our emotions run amok it would have been nice while it lasted. Wonderful. Amazing.

When I came out, however, clean and ready for the day, I continued our conversation as if we'd not spent the entire morning avoiding each other and the emotional baggage we seemed to be accumulating. I stuck my nose in the air and pretended to be casual. "You were wrong about one thing."

He looked up from grabbing his suitcase so we could leave and his expression was murderous. He fairly snapped his next words. "What was I wrong about?"

"We aren't semi-strangers. Not anymore." I huffed when I said it and stomped after him.

He deflated. His shoulders slumped and he said, wryly, "Agreed."

His voice was a bit less gruff as he set off with me following as I finished my little speech. "If we were strangers when we met, we aren't any longer. Not after sharing rooms and beds ever since leaving home and especially not after yesterday and last night."

We left the motel and walked into the bright light of day with me trailing behind and half running to keep up as he strode ahead without looking back with both of us pulling suitcases through town to the repair shop to see if his SUV was fixed.

It was and we drove back to town to a café for a meal that we lingered over much longer than necessary before heading north once more. Just north. And we didn't have to kiss or laugh or call upon any emotion at all to be able to sit in that café as long as we wished because the entity had listened to us and was giving us some slack.

It was about time.

We still had no inkling how much farther we'd have to travel. We'd agreed to take whatever small breaks we could now that we'd come to an understanding with the entity. We explained to it that we were exhausted and needed to recharge and meals were the perfect times for that. On a personal level, it felt like staking a claim to our humanity by lingering over coffee and pie instead of hurrying out to the SUV and so we stayed for a long time after each meal. Just because we could.

Later that day we were glad for the passports we'd brought with us without knowing exactly why because the compulsion drew us to the border between the USA and Canada, and then into the wilderness beyond.

And still we drove. North. We were being pulled towards a place we couldn't picture except in our minds. Our memories. Our dreams. We knew only that our destination was a lake surrounded by forest somewhere north of where we were.

Eventually, we found ourselves in surroundings that almost resembled our dreams. Not the lake itself. We passed many lakes but never that particular one. But the forest resembled the forest of our dreams and we were engulfed by the feel of that forest, the scent of it, the look of it when we stopped for lunch in a tiny Canadian town that wasn't even a dot on the map but had a country store with sandwiches we could heat up in their microwave and chocolate milk from the refrigerated section of the grocery aisle because we'd long since gone through the sandwich makings we'd brought from my house and also the additional makings purchased on the way.

We'd not used a map until then but we bought one so we could navigate the wilderness and plan a path from one small town to the next because there were so few towns that we'd have to time our arrivals if we wanted a place to eat and another to stay for the night.

North, of course, always north, but without the map we'd have had to sleep in the SUV. A couple days later, as late afternoon arrived, we scoured the map carefully for a place to spend the night. "I'd prefer to sleep in a bed. Not the SUV." Because it was looking like we'd not have much choice.

"Hopefully there will be something in the next town."

I put a finger on the map. "There." I pointed. "A town. It'll have something." A largish town, not large in comparison to the towns of our home country, but larger than the ones we'd gone through since crossing the border. "Surely it's large enough that there will be some place for us."

"Do you suppose we'll already have a reservation?"

"I don't know. I feel that we are close to our destination. So maybe there will be a reservation for us but perhaps, instead, we'll reach the end of our journey so we'll not need to sleep somewhere else tonight."

We looked at one another. We agreed we weren't ready to face the entity behind the compulsion even though we needed to end whatever was happening to us.

The town was called Deercreek and had a Bed and Breakfast and several resorts, plus a town square that was both quaint and efficient because the entire business district could be accessed from the square. It was clean and neat and gave off good vibes.

That was important, we told each other, because it might mean what we'd find at the end of our journey would also give off good vibes. It was nothing we could know for sure but something about the town felt right.

Good. Pleasant.

Jude agreed we were close to the end, though for a more practical reason. More than a feeling. "If we go much further north, we'll be in the arctic. Few roads and, eventually, the Arctic Ocean."

We weren't that far north according to the map. Not quite. There were still many miles before reaching the ocean but there was a distinct snap to the air and a clarity not felt elsewhere so, yes, we were definitely north.

"So now what?" Reaching the café where we planned to eat, Jude considered me. "We're close. No, not just close. We're here. I feel it."

"I feel it too. Deercreek is the place."

"But I don't get any vibe about where in Deercreek we're supposed to go. The entity isn't saying anything now. No compulsion. No direction."

"It's waiting."

"For us?"

"Possibly."

"Why isn't it helping us?"

"It said we could decide. Perhaps it's letting us do that."

"If so, it's smart move on the entity's part. It knows it can relent and end the compulsion and we'll still be likely to finish our journey if for no reason than that we've come this far so why not complete the journey."

"To see what we came all this way to find."

"But it's not telling us where it is. Why not?"

"Because it wants us to find it? To care enough to look for it?"

Jude turned grim. "No matter the reason, when we

find it, we'll stare it down and say some not nice things and take control of our destiny."

The finality of our decision to find the entity and discover why we'd made our journey settled around our shoulders like a physical weight. But it felt right.

We pushed open the door to the single café in town. We'd been in more cafes than we wanted to count on our journey but perhaps this one would be the last.

The walls were covered with local crafts, a stuffed moose head, crossed snowshoes, a birchbark canoe pretty much like the one in our dreams and a huge map of the area, complete with all the lakes and resorts in case people from out of town needed help locating a place.

"Nice map. It might be helpful. It would be if we knew what we were looking for." We ate lunch and left the café. We found a B&B with a vacancy for the night. "Just one night."

We told each other that the next day we would find the entity, then we pulled our suitcases inside and up a flight of stairs to the only room they had left. One bed. Just one. Of course, because why should this last night be any different from all the others?

We carefully avoided each other and with great willpower managed not to turn red. We politely took turns in the attached bathroom and slid into bed, unsure how to proceed. Because for once, oddly enough, there was no compulsion to fight. It was gone. Completely. But in it's place was a feeling. Nothing we could put a name to but it held a question. A wish to see the end of our journey. A curiosity. But it wasn't strong enough to distract us from the fact that we were once again sharing a bed. And the bed wasn't a King. Just a Queen.

"So how do we do now?" At least Jude had the sense to bring what we were both thinking into the open.

"I don't have a clue."

"We seem to have a thing about beds."

"At least it's a Queen. It could be a double bed."

Jude reached over once we were in bed and took my hand in his without moving closer. There was a slight distance between us so there was nothing romantic about the simple gesture but the act of holding hands sent my emotions into overdrive until I almost wished he'd not done it.

We stayed that way for a long time, then let our hands drop. We slid deep beneath the duvet and rolled away from each other, waiting to see if our emotions would get the better of us. Or for something to happen. Anything.

But nothing did except that eventually were able to sleep a full night without dreams of any kind or discomfort or even embarrassment and wake refreshed the next morning in the town we knew to be the end of our journey.

But we woke without a clue what to do next.

CHAPTER 10

We ate in the same café the next morning because there was no choice in the tiny town with Jude tipping his chair back on two legs as I'd learned was his habit. The waitress didn't approve but was too polite to say anything and Jude pretended not to get the message of her raised eyebrows. It was enjoyable to engage in such a normal thing and fun to watch her annoyance.

She saw us looking at the map on the wall and pretended she hadn't been annoyed at all. She actually smiled because we were obviously tourists and must be catered to though the smile was forced. "We have copies of the map at the checkout counter." She tipped her head towards a display case beside the cash register. "They are free compliments of the Chamber of Commerce. Saves having to tell people new to the area where to go." People like us. She rolled her eyes.

Her expression said she couldn't understand how anyone could get lost in a very small town or in the surrounding large and complex wilderness and we didn't enlighten her how easy it would be. I got a map and spread it over the table. Jude's chair came down with a thump and we examined it closely. "We're looking for a lake."

"There are a lot of them." The map was full of blue dots representing the many lakes in the area.

"Which is the one from our dreams?" We stared at the map as if it could tell us something.

And, oddly enough, it did.

Both Jude and I found our fingers touching the same lake on the map, the one with the town we were in at the south end. We could see it through the café window. The odd thing was that our fingers touched it on the map at the same time and we pulled back instantly and looked at each other.

No compulsion had pushed our fingers there, not that we could sense, anyway, but the memory of the lake in our dream was strong and only one lake on the map felt right. Looked right. The one that was blue and inviting just beyond the café window.

It was only a lake on a map but it was the one we sought. We both knew it with a certainty that left no doubt.

It was a very large lake. The largest in the area. It resembled a spider with bays and inlets going in all directions from the rather long and thin main part. Some of those bays and inlets were longer than the lake itself. Some were wide enough to almost be lakes themselves while others were spindly. Many went miles into the wilderness before becoming tiny creeks or swamps. It was appropriately named Spider Lake.

Jude said what we were both thinking. "That's the lake." The longer we stared at the map the more we knew the lake was the end of our journey.

"But it's huge. Where along the lake should we go?" Because we felt no compulsion. Nothing to tell us where to find the end of our journey.

"I guess we start looking."

"Let's ask the entity. If it actually wants us to find it before we die of old age it'll have to help." Not in the café, of course. People would think we were crazy because we'd be talking to thin air.

"When we are done eating. There's plenty of nearby forest. We can find a spot among the trees where no one will be watching and we can talk to the entity."

Our looks met in a kind of finality. We were close to the end of our journey. To the place where we'd finally discover what the journey was about. What the mission the entity mentioned entailed. Possibly, and most important of all, we'd learn if we truly had a choice as the entity had promised. If we did have that choice, if it hadn't been a lie, then we'd learn what our choices would include.

After breakfast we strolled casually to the edge of town so no one would notice and then wandered about until we found a thick grove of evergreens young enough that their branches still touched the ground and that, when we stepped behind them, gave us complete and utter privacy. We looked to each other for confidence.

Jude had done the bulk of the work during our journey. He'd kept us both going and kept me sane. It was my turn now so I took the initiative. I cleared my throat and had to make myself speak because it was strange talking to thin air. "Entity, we are at the right lake but we don't know where to find you. You must tell us where to go."

Nothing. Not a sound, not a thought, not a whisper in our minds. So Jude tried. "Hey, Entity. How about a little guidance here? You're in a hurry so I doubt you want us stumbling around like a couple of idiots looking for you and not finding you." He added in a mutter that only I could hear, "Especially since we don't know what you look like so wouldn't know you if we ran you over with the SUV."

Still nothing. We stayed in that small, thick grove, talking, yelling, asking for guidance for over an hour before giving up and returning to the town square where we dropped to a bench along a path frequented by elderly men, small children and dogs. "What now?"

"We go home." Jude's voice was petulant. "It obviously doesn't care anymore."

I thought about that. "If we start home, will we get there? Or will the compulsion return and force us to turn around and come back north?"

"We told it we need help and it ignored us. It doesn't care anymore. Maybe it changed its mind." A shrug said Jude didn't know any more than I did.

Jude broke a blossom from a nearby bush and slid it over my ear. It tickled and smelled like summer and his eyes said he liked the way it looked.

"I think we should keep looking because we don't want to get part of the way home and have to turn around when the compulsion comes roaring back."

He sighed agreement. "If we don't find the entity in a day or so, then we can head home."

We were too restless to sit longer so we took a tour around the town square, holding hands and walking slowly to take in the small town ambiance of the place. It was dotted with benches, most empty, but a few with people relaxing in the middle of the day. A small boy, possibly eight or so, sat on a bench with a large cardboard box on the bench beside him. In the box were two puppies.

"Hey, Mister." He snagged Jude as we walked past. "Want a puppy? It's free."

Jude was closest to the boy but as soon as the boy spoke, he slipped around me so I was between him and the puppies and he stayed that way. I was a bulwark between him and two cute puppies. He pointed to me. "She's the puppy person. She loves them. She raises them."

"Not that kind of puppies." I frowned ferociously. "Service dogs. And I have all I want, thank you very much." I stared him down, ignoring his grin that told the boy that of course I'd take a puppy as he kept me between those cute puppies and himself.

The boy's eye lit up. "You'll take one?" He ignored my head shaking to tell him I didn't want one. He retrieved the two puppies, one in each hand, and held them up. They were adorable because all puppies are adorable. One was black with white splattered over its body and the other was white with black splatters. "I can't take a puppy now. I'm going somewhere and I don't know if they allow dogs."

The boy's eyes misted. "If no one takes them soon, bad things will happen to them." He held the puppies close to my face so I couldn't ignore them. "Pleeese."

Jude's silent laughter said he knew what was going to happen next and he was right. I scowled at him fiercely as I took first one puppy, then the other. Not because I was agreeing to anything. Just because they were cute and were in danger if no one adopted them. Besides, they wiggled in the boy's hands. He might drop them and I couldn't let that happen.

Then Jude spoke. "We can use a little happiness right now." He sounded wistful.

My shoulders slumped. "And puppies qualify."

"You should know. But I can't have a dog. I'm gone too much." He tickled the puppies beneath their chins. "You have a fenced in yard and you have puppies all the time." His look begged me to take one. Or both. "You can give them a home. I can't."

Five minutes later we carried both puppies and their box to Jude's SUV where we tucked them in behind us and cracked a window so they'd have fresh air. I studied Jude as I examined them carefully to make sure they were comfortable and had access to the food and water that had been part of the puppy package. "You're not immune to dogs."

He gave me a sheepish look. "I'd have one if I could." He checked the puppies one last time. "Or two. I'm glad they'll have a good home."

"Do you suppose the entity likes dogs?"

"Who knows? It's not human. Maybe it eats dogs."

"I hope not."

We were in the SUV and unfolding the map with the lake that was the right one, a fact we knew with a certainty that couldn't be denied though the knowing was intuitive rather than intellectual. When the map was spread across our knees Jude touched the lake and said thoughtfully, "I don't think the entity eats dogs."

"I agree and how do we both know that when we can't possibly know anything about the entity?'

He knew where my thoughts were going. "Because perhaps we know more about this mysterious entity than we realize?"

The idea gave us pause. "I agree. We do know a lot

about it. But where did that knowledge come from? It never gave clues about itself."

"Yes it did. We know things. We know that our relationship with the entity is more intimate than we'd realized. More intimate than we wished it to be. More complicated. Somehow I believe we've connected with it in a way so subtle we've not realized it was happening."

"I never thought of that but you're right." I didn't know if I liked the idea of being connected to something that couldn't be human but I couldn't deny that I was.

Jude continued slowly. "The fact that we are more in tune with the entity than we realized is why we are going to find it even though the compulsion is gone. It's why we're not turning around and heading home."

"Because somehow, in some way we can't understand, we know it's not evil."

"And because we are curious." He smiled. "Curiosity killed the cat."

"We want to know what took control of us. What brought us on what may turn out to be a wild goose chase."

"We want to know what speaks to our minds and listens when we talk to it out loud."

"We want to know why it believes we are in love."

"And how it gave us dreams."

I thought back to the dreams we no longer had. "A deer and its fawn. Blue sky. A rural road. A green forest. And a lake that, somehow, over the course of all those dreams, was the one we recognized when we saw it on a map."

Jude gave a long sigh. "We can only hope we don't

end up like that curious cat."

We glanced at the map again and the knowledge that we were on the right path sent goosebumps along my spine. It was a knowledge that grew stronger as we looked at the map. The lake was the right lake. We were in the right place and near the end of our journey.

We climbed into the SUV and looked through the windshield at the lake before us and the town that hugged its southern tip. Somewhere along that lakeshore was the home of the entity that had been calling to us. All we had to do now was to pinpoint where on that lake it lived.

Jude drove along the shore but after while he pulled off the road and we stared at the blue water that reflected a blue sky. We watched small waves smoothing out as the breeze died. We waited for knowledge to come, for something to tell us where to go. But nothing happened. "There's no more compulsion. No direction. Nothing to tell us where to go."

Jude touched the south end of the lake on the map I had spread across my knees. "The town is here. The north end of the lake is wilderness so there's not likely anything there. But there are lots of resorts between the town and the wilderness. Lots of roads. A few small farms."

I folded the map. "Common sense says the most likely place to find anyone – or anything – is where there are roads and buildings so we start our search near town and if we don't find the entity we'll spread out from there."

"How will we recognize it? We don't know what it looks like."

"We'll know. Somehow." We agreed that we would, indeed, know it when we saw it.

Three days later we were no closer to finding the entity than when we began our search, though we were totally in love with two puppies. So were the dog-loving owners of the B&B we kept staying in for one more night and then still another one and one more after that because we still hadn't found what we were looking for.

They were more than happy to allow two puppies in our room though they were definite that they didn't need any more dogs because they had enough. Pete and Repeat, as we called them, had quickly become part of our lives and loved to travel in their big, cardboard box in the back seat of the SUV as we spent hours and then days driving along every one of the many gravel roads at the south end of the lake in search of something we'd recognize when we found it.

The pups soon sported lovely handmade collars attached to matching handmade leashes that we bought at highly inflated prices in the laid-back tourist town that was still much like it had been a hundred years ago.

We looked forward to the day the puppies would be able to do their business on command and knew we'd need patience in the meantime. Jude was fascinated by everything about the art of raising puppies and wished he could have one of his own. But his job wouldn't allow it.

By then, everyone in the tiny town knew us and wondered at our endless driving along the gravel roads that spread out like a spider's web through the forest around the web shaped lake. We suspected they got together when we weren't around and laughed loud and long at the weird tourists who couldn't decide what they wanted even with a map to help. We were glad they were polite enough not to laugh in our faces.

After almost a week of searching we'd still not found the entity. "Nor have we found the part of the lake we saw in our dreams."

"It was quite specific." A bay with a tangle of logs at one end and a tiny sand beach curving along the edge of the water that sparkled when the sun hit it just right. No place we'd seen so far had a beach resembling the one in our dreams though there was a rather large beach near the town where everyone swam during the few weeks of the summer when the water was warm enough for hardy souls to jump in. "The forest in our dreams was thicker, I think. And there was a rather large hill in the background."

"I haven't seen any hills. It's flat as a pancake around here so the entity's home should be easy to locate by the hill alone. If we find a hill, we find the entity."

"That's a big 'if.'"

"The strange light came from the hill. It was a rather large, high hill."

We stared at the map spread over the table in our room in the B&B. "We've been everywhere and there are no hills. We'd have seen it by now if there was one."

"We haven't been to the wilderness part of the lake. It must be at the far end of the lake." We poured over the map. "There's only one road beyond the areas with resorts and houses."

"Why is that?"

"And why are all the resorts and houses at the

south end?" I peered at it as if it would tell us something. "Why are there none at the north end?"

We asked the owners of the B&B. "No one knows much about the lake except here near town."

"Why is that?"

"Because one person owns everything around the lake except right near town. He owns hundreds of acres. Maybe thousands. Just one old man. Can you imagine that? And he's a hermit."

CHAPTER 11

"Do you know him?"

"No one knows him. He shows up in town now and then. Like I said, he's a hermit. A nice enough old guy, I suppose, but he never stays long. Just picks up supplies and he orders ahead so he doesn't even go into the stores. He has someone load his truck and then he's gone."

The owner of the B&B thought a bit. "Though it's kind of funny. As far as we know he lives alone because we've never seen anyone with him. But he buys enough supplies to keep an army in food and comfort for a long time."

He turned back to making dinner. We'd interrupted with our questions. Lovely smells wafted to us as he lifted the lid of one pot after another. "Perhaps he has a lot of company. That could explain the supplies though we don't see many vehicles going in that direction. Not any, actually, except his truck when he comes to town. But maybe they come and we don't notice. Or maybe he buys food for the wild animals. The deer and such. Some people feed them. Think they can't survive without help." A snort said what he thought of that possibility.

Jude and I looked at one another, our eyes wide. Both of our hearts stopped and then speeded up because the old man – the hermit -- was the entity. He must be. Jude spoke to me but was heard by the B&B owner checking his pots. "It's him. The hermit is the entity."

"Entity?" The lid slammed down on a pot and the owner turned to us. We were surely insane. His expression said he just might kick us out of his B&B out of concern for the safety of his other guests.

Jude pretended he'd made a joke and the B&B owner relaxed slightly and when we were alone we reminded ourselves that we'd better watch what we said. It was so recently that the compulsion had actually allowed us to interact with other people that we'd not got used to mentally monitoring our speech.

So after some discussion we checked out of the B&B and said we'd not be returning. The owner seemed relieved. "No sense taking chances on saying something wrong again. He'll have us committed for sure. If we don't find the entity today surely some resort will have a vacant cabin. A cabin will have privacy. We won't have to talk with anyone."

"We won't need a cabin. We won't need anything. We'll find the entity today."

"And then what?"

We stared at each other. "I don't know."

Jude wrapped an arm around my shoulder where it lay warm and heavy. "When we see what we have to deal with, we'll know what to do. Stay or head home."

"If we really do have a choice. If he – it -- doesn't use some kind of magic to prevent us from leaving."

"It won't be able to stop us." Jude meant what he said and if his fierceness could overcome the compulsion then we'd be safe. That and the protective way his arm lay over my shoulder, sharing his certainty. "Whether we find the entity or not we won't need a cabin or B&B or any place in this area to spend the night."

"Because if we don't find what we're looking for we'll be gone. South. Not north, we'll be going south. We'll be on way our home."

"Or we'll be with the entity."

We bought the makings of lunch in case our search took a long time plus a supply of puppy food and a couple gallon jugs of water. We packed everything as carefully in the SUV as if we were preparing for a major expedition when all we were doing was taking a seldom used road around the large, spider-shaped lake.

It was a road that led to a wilderness with no houses, no other roads and, according to the owner of the B&B, only one somewhat unusual old man.

We had no idea what to expect and I was terrified. Jude not so much. He was excited.

Soon after we turned onto that road we left civilization behind. Though we were still close to the town, it was as if we'd stepped into another world because that road, unlike the others, was hardly travelled at all though it was well maintained. But it was narrow and barely more than dirt.

The forest was the same forest that surrounded the town, the birds and unseen animals that scurried away as we drove slowly along the seldom used gravel road were similar to the ones around the town. But something was different, something we couldn't quite describe or even understand but the difference screamed at us.

Jude slowed and coasted to the side of the road until the SUV came to a stop. He didn't say anything but he didn't have to. I knew what he was thinking. "This is the right road. I know it is. And I'm scared to death."

We got out and looked around. We walked away from the SUV. I tipped my head and examined the trees meeting overhead. "There's no question that it's the right road." Because in our dreams we'd traveled a road with trees that met overhead exactly as the trees above us.

Jude took my hand because right then we needed each other. We were nearing the end. We were afraid and awed and eager all at the same time so we held hands like small children in a new and unfamiliar place, giving each other the courage to continue. Like Hansel and Gretel.

For a long time we stood on that road, looking around, listening to muted sounds and taking in verdant smells as we watched the tops of those tall evergreens swaying peacefully in the breeze that was so high up that the tops of the trees might as well have been in the sky while no air moved at ground level because the forest grew too thickly to allow any air at all to move so low. "The trees must be hundreds of years old. Or thousands."

"This whole area belongs to one man. Miles and miles of it and nothing has ever been logged. It must be a multi-generational piece of land and each generation refused all offers to log it off. So it's still primeval."

"Like a church."

Jude's next words broke the spell that until then had held us in thrall. "I somehow doubt the entity is familiar with churches, at least not the kind we know." We laughed and returned to the SUV.

The puppies yipping said they needed time out of their box. We took them on leashes and they sniffed everything eagerly, tails wagging so hard their bodies wagged too, and their ears flipped back and forth at the wilderness sounds.

When their antics slowed and they'd done their business so perhaps wouldn't need to go again and thus create a need for their box to be cleaned and a new layer of towels laid in the bottom to replace the ones that would need to be washed when we reached a place with a laundry, we dropped them back into their box. They curled around each other and promptly fell asleep and we were able to continue.

"I hope we didn't make a mistake by bringing the puppies. I hope the entity won't be angry."

"I doubt it eats puppies. It didn't feel like a puppy-eating entity. No puppy-eating vibes." That statement was about more than puppies. It said we were accepting what we were doing. That we weren't about to turn around and run. That we believed whatever lay ahead either would be decent. That we would survive.

Jude drove slowly, then still slower as the SUV went farther and deeper into the wilderness. I tried to track our movements on the map but was unable to do so because it was all the same. Evergreens. Ferns along the forest floor. Birds zooming across the occasional breaks in the trees. And unseen animals watching as we passed.

Eventually, we were barely moving.

"You're afraid," I said quietly.

The excitement Jude had felt earlier was gone,

replaced by a different emotion. "Terrified."

We continued on. "There are no side roads. No logging trails."

"Just the one road and it goes straight to the entity."

Jude drove slower and slower still until we were creeping at a walking pace along the gravel road that grew narrower as we drove. "Soon it'll disappear. There won't be any road at all."

"Because we'll be there?"

A curve lay ahead. As we came around that gentle curve, the evergreens opened onto a large clearing with a huge log building in the foreground and numerous other log buildings of various sizes, some almost as large as the main building, behind it, scattered in such a way that no one building was close to any other.

As Jude had predicted, the road petered out until it was a driveway and then it disappeared entirely into a neatly mowed yard that encompassed the entire extremely large clearing with both evergreen and hardwood trees scattered throughout. It was lovely and not a soul could be seen anywhere.

"Guess we go find someone." Jude climbed out of the SUV and came around to my side. I was still inside, afraid to open the door, afraid to step out, afraid to find out the truth of this place we'd spent so much time reaching.

As Jude helped me out, something happened.

A door in the main building opened slowly. It was a huge double door, only one side of which swung out. A man stood in the doorway, an elderly man, neither tall nor short, with silver hair and a slight stoop, but as he advanced and crossed the wide porch that wrapped entirely around the building, and then came down the broad stairs, he moved slowly and with difficulty. He was either very tired or quite ill.

He came closer. Waved to us to come forward as if coming all the way to us would tax his body more than was wise. We carefully approached him.

We both recognized him at the same time. "Lourdes Jones." Two words because they were all that we could say. The man from the service dog convention. Of course it was him. We'd suspected as much.

He smiled at me, that blinding, sweet simile I remembered. "Welcome, lovely lady who loves puppies." He half bowed with the same courtesy he'd showed that first day of the convention and each of the remaining days.

He turned to Jude. "And you, too. The consummate jet pilot." He examined us both, the smile breaking across his face as bright as the sun that poured down on us all and growing larger with each passing second. He smiled in spite of the illness or fatigue or whatever it was that enveloped him. "I'm so glad to see you both. I was afraid you'd not make it. That you couldn't find it. I'm afraid I've not been well so I wasn't able to help you during this last leg of your journey. I was too fragile to go into town and meet you."

He sighed. "As you no doubt noticed, recently and a few times during your journey, I was unable to communicate with you. It was the illness, I'm afraid, and I apologize. But I'm slowly getting better, though old age makes everything more difficult." He smiled wanly. "Old age is unforgiving, I'm afraid."

He waved us towards the building and slowly, with

effort, turned around to lead the way inside. He was so different from at the service dog convention. So tired. So ill. But he gathered what strength he could summon and motioned us to follow. "Come with me."

He waved to us a second time as if afraid we wouldn't follow him. "Come in and have some tea." He paused a moment. "It's excellent. I promise. I do like a good cup of tea."

He took the first steps towards the building and Jude and I followed hesitantly. "We'll talk over tea," he said as he made his painful way up the stairs. He stopped to rest halfway up though this time not turning back to make sure we were following, possibly because his effort so far had been all he could manage and he was close to being worn out completely. "There's a lot to explain and I'm sure you are eager to hear what all this is about."

I lagged behind the two men. Jude, however, was eager to put an end to our quest. And to help an elderly man. He quickly caught up to Lourdes Jones and helped him up the stairs and across the porch. I felt guilty at ignoring Lourdes but I was still held by the fear that had taken a firm hold of me the moment we'd turned onto the forest road that had led us here.

The fear hadn't dissipated and kept me from moving too close to the man from the service dog convention who was clearly not who I'd thought he was. Or *what* I'd thought he was.

I was in awe of Jude for being able to overcome those same fears and help a frail, elderly man – or being of some kind -- across a porch and into a very large and quite elegant log building with a huge main room with a rock fireplace that covered an entire wall that was at least three stories high. Yet we sensed that this was just one room of a building that went on forever, going much farther back on the property than what we'd been able to see from the front. It was simply awesome.

Lourdes Jones waved an arm, a slight movement that I was sure would have been robust had he been feeling better, and a trolley appeared with a teapot and a selection of cups, saucers, teaspoons and everything else needed for tea, plus what appeared to be a tray of delicate cookies and candies. No one pushed the trolley. It merely came towards us of its own volition. A shiver went along my spine because it shouldn't be happening.

It reached Lourdes and he grabbed it with a light touch and redirected it towards where we were walking, a smaller room behind the huge room we were in. It went ahead of us. We followed silently and soon found ourselves in what would have been called a sitting room in another time and a different world, one with lords and ladies and wait staff with harp music in the background.

There was no central table. Instead, there were comfortable chairs scattered about with small tables to hold teacups with brightly colored rugs here and there and light colored drapes at the windows pulled wide to let the sun pour through and the windows were so huge that even though it was a log building that would normally be quite dark inside, it was full of the brightness of the outside world. It was lovely and the yellow décor that seemed to be everywhere added to that brightness and made the whole room feel right. And homey. And safe.

None of which made any difference to me. I was terrified and it was all I could do not to turn around and run outside and keep running until I was home and safe from whatever was about to happen.

CHAPTER 12

Lourdes Jones poured tea into elegant cups and handed them to us. Jude's cup looked ridiculously small in his large, male hands but Lourdes was the epitome of the old-world charm that had entranced me at the service dog convention. He offered us sugar and lemon. Neither Jude nor I accepted. We were beyond thinking about such things.

Lourdes leaned back in a tired way, took a sip of tea, and smiled. Then he moved forward and set his cup on the nearest small, marble table. "I apologize for you two having to find me." He shrugged, a motion every bit as elegant as everything else so far had been. "If I'd have communicated in the way I'd done earlier, through dreams or mental cognition in order to tell you how to find this place once you reached Deercreek, the force of the communication would have been so strong as to have blown you away. You were too close, you see. The signal would have been too much. Too loud." He tut-tutted. "It's a human thing, I suppose, not being able to handle the audio or mental load if it's close. Part and parcel of the frailty of humans. And I was too tired to think of a different way. Too sick."

I took a sip of my tea in imitation of Lourdes

because sipping tea was evidently what we were doing as I tried to take in what he'd said. He'd called us human. He hadn't included himself in that description, exactly, but he hadn't precluded himself from the human race, either. I decided I didn't care about signals that might or might not overwhelm us. I only cared about the other part of his explanation. The human part.

I pointed to him. "You're human." It was a question though without the inflection.

He stared at his tea for a long time before answering in an apologetic voice. "Actually, I'm not."

My breath stopped. "You're not human?"

Jude made a strangled sound in his throat and when he spoke it most definitely wasn't a question. It wasn't even polite. It was a bald statement. An accusation. "You're not human."

Lourdes waved aside our words with fingers that trailed absentmindedly through the air. "I accept that I do look human. Or, if you look at it from my viewpoint, humans look a lot like my species. But looks can be deceiving."

Another sip of tea delayed his next statement. After a moment, though, he set his cup on the table and leaned back, closed his eyes, and enjoyed the aftertaste of what I was sure must be expensive, specialty tea. I'd not know the difference but I was sure he did. "Most species in this galaxy look human. Or somewhat human. Humanoid, I believe is the proper term."

"They look like us." This time my words weren't a question, they were a stunned statement of something I now knew to be true though they spoke to a fact I was having a hard time wrapping my mind around. Lourdes Jones wasn't human. Furthermore he was acquainted with various species that lived elsewhere than Earth and those species, according to him, also resembled human beings.

The elderly man smiled at me gently. I felt like a gauche child and was glad for the temporary silence that let me absorb this information.

Jude was way ahead of me. The part of his mind that brought jet planes to wherever they needed to get to safely because he could think on his feet and react instantaneously had grabbed onto the fact that Lourdes had mentioned the galaxy as if it was the next town over and that it was filled with other species.

Unlike me, though, he wasn't knocked on his keister by the information. Instead he blinked in a way that said he was assessing the information. Then he inspected Lourdes much the same way Lourdes had just inspected us. Politely. "Why is that, do you suppose? That so many species look similar." As if this was an ordinary, everyday conversation and how could both Lourdes and Jude be so casual about it? I was amazed by both of them.

Then I looked hard at Jude. He spoke normally but his fingers around his cup were white from holding it so hard. I feared it would shatter but somehow it didn't. Another odd thing about our situation. Were the teacups impervious to breakage? They looked delicate but obviously weren't. What were they made of?

Lourdes shrugged, his thin shoulders moving slowly and with effort. His health had declined shockingly since the service dog convention. "Who knows why? Convergent evolution? Seeding of similar life on various planets? No one knows, actually. We only know that intelligent life throughout the galaxy is similar enough in appearance to allow for interspecies intermingling. On a social level, at least. And social interactions are nice, don't you think? They are so civilized." He sighed. "I like civilized species."

Lourdes raised his teacup and took another sip. A genteel gesture. "I do so enjoy our being together here and now." He waved his hand to take in the tea things and the room and the general ambiance. "It's such a pleasant experience, is it not? The tea is excellent and the company is sublime."

Then Lourdes, instead of sighing and taking another sip of tea and making another statement that would blow our world apart, closed his eyes and leaned back wearily. Seeing his obvious exhaustion I was ashamed of myself for not saying anything earlier. "Have you been seriously ill?"

Jude was also sorry for having ignored our host's appearance. "You are tired. At the service dog convention, you weren't like this."

Lourdes opened his eyes but stayed supine. "Yes, I'm afraid I have been ill. A human virus and, not being human, it's affected me more than would normally be expected. And, yes, it's put a damper on what I've been attempting to accomplish with you two and because of that, everything has been somewhat crudely done."

He sat up then and pulled strength from somewhere inside of him. He snapped his fingers and the trolley moved close. He touched it and it left the room and disappeared. Then he gathered still more strength and sat taller in that lovely, embroidered chair and extended his hands towards us in what we recognized as a polite gesture from another era.

"I do apologize for not meeting you in town. That

was my original plan once I realized your human bodies couldn't handle the full strength of the communication method that seems to be the only one that can be counted on to work with humans."

"You're talking about the compulsion."

"That's what you call it?" He seemed to think that over and nodded that it sounded right. "And the dreams. Two sides of the same coin, the dreams and the compulsion as you call it. I always start with dreams because they are a very human thing."

He seemed to drift into thought for a moment and I recalled the peaceful nature of the dreams. "But eventually I accepted the need for something more specific because humans can – and do – ignore their dreams."

He shook his head as if bypassing dreams meant we'd missed out on something. "I had to use another method in addition to the dreams and I decided upon what you call the compulsion."

He looked from one of us to the other with a sheepish expression. "I didn't realize at the time how strongly it would affect you." He rubbed his forehead in vexation. "I'd have used a different method if I'd have known that but, to be honest, I couldn't then and still can't think of another method that would work." He added, "With humans, that is."

"We followed the compulsion as you wanted us to and we came north. We found you." Jude's bald statement cut through Lourdes' careful words. He was about to say something about our being treated as puppets on a string. I knew he was thinking that and that he was about to let Lourdes know how we felt about his tactics.

Before he could speak, though, Lourdes drooped a bit and rubbed his forehead wearily with a hand and Jude relented and quietly said, "We're sorry you don't feel well."

Lourdes nodded. "It's like I said. An Earthly thing. A bug, no doubt. Don't know what, exactly. Probably something I caught at the convention. Or on the way home. And I'm old. Old people – old beings of any species – don't have the strength to fight illnesses the way young beings do."

He thought over his words. "Home being subjective, of course, because this lovely place you see around us is my home on Earth but, of course my true home – my place of origin – is many light years away."

"Of course it is." What else could we say?

Jude's comment was intentionally sarcastic and Lourdes' lips turned up slightly. Not enough to be a smile but it was close. "I see you have a sense of humor. Sarcasm can be a type of humor that helps humans deal with unusual situations and I believe this qualifies.

"I understand that this is a shock to both of you and humor is an excellent way to alleviate surprise." His lips turned up still more. "It's one of the human traits I'm especially fond of."

He closed his eyes once more and gave a sigh of contentment as he sank a bit lower in the brocade chair that did, indeed, look comfortable. "Which proves that my assessment of you two at the service dog convention was correct. You are the right people for the job." He opened his eyes wide and looked straight at us. "If you choose to accept it."

We froze at his mention of a choice being given to

us but instead of expanding on that he returned to the subject of our arrival. "I apologize still again for not meeting you in town. I was simply not up to it physically."

What could we say? He wasn't up to much at all. He'd barely been able to meet us when we arrived.

Just then a yipping drifted through the open window. Pete and Repeat were awake and wanted attention. Jude and I looked at each other and didn't know what to say or do but Lourdes had heard the sound. "What's that?" His eyes went round. Clearly the sound of very young puppies was foreign to him.

"Uh .." I sought to explain. "In the last town, the one at the south end of the lake, there's a town square — "

He nodded that he knew about the square and I went on to explain in clumsy words about the boy and the box with two puppies in it that needed a home. Before I finished my tale, he threw back his head and laughed in delight and some of his weariness disappeared, at least momentarily, as he said, "And as we speak, those very puppies that you rescued from a fate worse than death are in your vehicle and wanting attention."

His eyes snapped with enjoyment at what I assumed he saw as still another very human thing. "Your action with the puppies is more proof of what I just said. That you two are the right people for the job. Your reaction to small beings of another species that are in potential trouble is precisely what is needed for the job I have in mind for you."

He tried to see out the window but the SUV was in front of the building and the windows were on one side.

"You care about beings belonging to other species than your own. In your case, it's dogs. In the years I've been here, I've met more different species than you can possibly imagine and all of them have been wonderful and interesting. But none can possibly be as cute as puppies."

He asked us to bring the puppies into the sunshine yellow room but I hesitated. "They are not housebroken."

When I explained what that meant, he waved an arm in what I'd already figured was part of his personality – or a deliberate gesture that could produce specific results – and said it didn't matter. "The young of any species are delightful creatures. I'm sure there won't be any problems while they are here. Bring them to me. Please."

He relapsed back into the tired old man we'd seen when we first arrived as we did as he asked, bringing both the puppies and their box into the bright room. We figured the box would come in handy if they had accidents.

We could use the towels from the box to clean up whatever needed cleaning and use the extra towels we'd brought along to replace the ones used so the puppies could still be comfortable. When it happened Lourdes would realize that, though they were cute, they were, after all, puppies.

Lourdes loved Pete and Repeat. That fact was evident in the way he stared at them with gleaming eyes and very carefully picked them up, first one and then the other. Then he put them both on his lap in a wiggly puppy pile while Jude and I waited with bated breath for one or the other to have an accident and ruin

Lourdes clothes. They appeared very expensive and I could only hope they could be laundered.

But that never happened. I wanted to ask if somehow Lourdes had charmed the puppies in much the same way he'd charmed me and then Jude at the convention which must also be how he'd used thought control over inanimate objects such as the trolley that now hung at the back of the room and waited to be given a command. I had no doubt that if Lourdes snapped his fingers it would respond.

And it did. It soon brought what I assumed were puppy treats and Pete and Repeat were soon tussling with each other on what I was sure was an expensive oriental rug over which got the treat they each wanted even though there were plenty go around and all were identical.

They never had an accident. And I never asked Lourdes if he was the reason because it would sound ridiculous. Puppies were puppies and how could a non-human from someplace far away in the galaxy control their bodily functions? Except I was sure he had.

It soon became clear that Lourdes would gladly play with the puppies forever, but it was equally clear that he was growing weary. I took them gently from him and replaced them in their box, hoping against hope they'd be quiet. Lourdes peered at them in the box and waved one hand over them. And they promptly went to sleep.

I didn't question whether he'd done it or how because of course he'd put them to sleep. He'd used magic or whatever he used. There was no question about it. I was merely grateful that the puppies had been welcome. And they had been. Lourdes was clearly in love with them. Two small dogs.

I could only hope that love – or something close to it -- would also include Jude and me and whatever his plans for us involved.

CHAPTER 13

Lourdes wouldn't let us return the puppies to Jude's SUV. "No, no, no! They belong here." He looked around. "Don't you agree? This place needs a couple of puppies. I can't believe I didn't figure that out long ago, especially after my trip to the service dog convention."

The trolley led the way to a small room off the kitchen. It was the perfect place for two small critters, near the source of food and also close to the place where people were likely to be found. Though, as to that, I wasn't sure people actually used the kitchen. Maybe entities I couldn't imagine? Or perhaps the trolley did everything.

But Lourdes made it clear I could cook or bake or do whatever I chose. "I love the thought humans put into meals," he said in a somewhat mystified voice as he made sure the box that was the puppies' kennel was placed to one side where they could look into the kitchen through a glass door that might have been there all along though there weren't any other glass doors that I could see in the building.

Had the trolley built one as we sat in the bright yellow room and drank tea? Probably. The puppies slept as Lourdes waved his hand again and the trolley trundled along the floor with puppy food that couldn't possibly have existed before we arrived.

Then Lourdes turned to us. Weariness was evident in the movement, more so than when we'd arrived. He was wearing out fast. "I believe I need a rest." Of course he did. He waved a hand again. I saw nothing obvious happening but was sure something was being done somewhere because surely that's what Lourdes' waves were about. "I've made sure you will have adequate accommodation. I put much thought into how humans prefer their living quarters and I believe you'll be pleased."

Another wave in the direction of the trolley. "Dinner is whenever you are hungry. As for me, I believe I'll have something in my room but when you are ready to eat you can come back to the kitchen and tell the trolley what you want. Or you can prepare it yourself. The kitchen is well equipped and there's a pantry to one side. I made sure it was well stocked in anticipation of your arrival."

He turned away, then back. "We'll talk tomorrow. In the meantime, just follow the trolley to your rooms." And he was gone.

The silence of his leaving was deafening and we didn't know what to do next until Jude strolled over to the trolley and said, "Take us to our rooms," pretty much as an alien might tell earthlings to be taken to their leader. His words were awkward and stilted. And we waited to see what would happen.

The trolley moved, going slow enough for us to follow. Through the huge main front room with the fireplace to the three story hallway with a wide staircase leading to the upper floors. Somehow – we never knew how – the trolley ascended the stairs, rolling smoothly upwards while waiting with what I thought might be impatience as we, too, climbed the stairs, turning every few steps to take in the enormity and the grandeur of the place. No one in the nearby town knew it existed. Who had it been built to impress?

The trolley stopped on the second floor and trundled along the hall to the first door on the right. Somehow – and once again, we had no idea how it did it – it opened the door without touching it and led the way inside where it rolled to the center of a very large room and stopped.

"I think it's waiting for us to thank it for showing us our rooms."

"Maybe it wants a tip?" Jude's joke should have fallen flat but I giggled because it was totally appropriate at that moment. I'd already figured Jude had great situational awareness. When the trolley ignored his joke he told it politely that we could take it from there and the trolley rotated one hundred eighty degrees and left, shutting the door behind it.

We looked around. "More than one room. It's a suite and large enough to pass for a luxury apartment in any hotel in the world."

"Thank goodness because there are two of us." And we'd not only slept in the same motel rooms during our journey we'd also slept in the same bed. It was about time we got a bit of privacy.

"Let's check it out."

There was a bathroom larger than my bedroom at home and what we decided must be a sitting room complete with several chairs and small tables similar to those of the yellow room that I was convinced had been created for a tea party. The sitting room overlooked the yard and nearby forest while sun-dappled rays warmed the floor. There was also an office with two desks complete with computers and all the other usual office equipment.

The last room, past the others, was the bedroom and it was huge. Jude stood stock still in the middle of it. He looked for another door to indicate another bedroom. There was none. "One bedroom. Just one."

"With one bed. Just one."

"Can we ask for two bedrooms?"

We both shook our heads at the same time. "Nope. Won't work. Lourdes has decided we are a couple and we're stuck with that fact." We didn't know whether to laugh or cry.

"Tomorrow at that meeting I'll mention that human men and women don't usually sleep together unless they are married."

"Think he'll buy it?"

"Nope." Of course he wouldn't. "He's been playing matchmaker since we met. Why stop now?"

We checked out the walk-in closet that was a bit larger than the bathroom that was huge by our standards. Our luggage was neatly stacked at one end and the contents had been hung. Of course whatever had done the hanging hadn't differentiated between Jude's and my things so they were hung randomly.

Jude's comment was wry. "At least it's neat."

"We can separate our stuff." I examined the closet. "Which side do you want?"

He shrugged. "Whichever." Then he started to laugh.

Soon I was laughing with him and we never did separate our things. "Who knows what'll happen tomorrow? Maybe it won't matter because when we find out what this is all about we'll leave in a huff. With or without our luggage."

"Think he'll let us leave now that we know what he is?" We sobered quickly because we didn't know the answer.

Since we'd not rearrange the closet and there was nothing to do in our upscale suite except stare at the huge bed, we decided to return to the kitchen and contemplate dinner.

We found the kitchen without the help of the trolley but it was waiting for us when we entered and we heard the yipping of the puppies in the adjoining room. We checked on them and played with them until they fell asleep in our arms and we deposited them onto what we noticed were fresh, fluffy towels in their box. We found scissors in the kitchen that we used to cut one side so they could enter and exit their box at will. Then we headed to the kitchen proper to see about something to eat.

Lourdes had spoken truth when he said the kitchen was well stocked and so was the pantry. We chose the most expensive steaks of the many choices available and baked potatoes while wondering how he managed to have fresh food of any kind when he shopped in town so seldom. But we didn't wonder long. We were past wondering anything about this place.

A little exploration revealed a grill on a patio beyond the kitchen and Jude turned out to be a grill chef, which was good because I'd have fried them in a pan. Jude shuddered with horror. "How can you even think about treating such gourmet food so callously?"

When we were done, we found a dishwasher in the kitchen. "Thank goodness. I was afraid we'd have to ask the trolley to clean up after us and, somehow, that just isn't something I wish to do."

"You mean it's not something you wish to do *yet*," Jude finished for me. "Who knows what we'll be doing if we stay here long enough."

"Does that mean you expect us to stay here for a long time?"

There was no appropriate answer to my question because we had no idea what our future held, but we found we could no longer joke around or play with the puppies we'd brought onto the patio while we ate since they'd waked from their nap. Because suddenly the future hung heavy over us. And turned us silent.

I glanced out the window to discover that even the weather seemed to be changing to accommodate our concerns. After putting the puppies back to bed and making sure the kitchen was clean, we went back outside because it was the north woods and the smells and sounds were calming and normal. Most important was the normal part.

But during our few minutes inside, clouds had slowly drifted across the sky and turned the porcelain blue sky to a foreboding gray. "Like in a movie," I said, wrapping my arms around my middle to keep me warm because I was suddenly chilled and, though I still wanted to be outside and feel the fresh air and smell the pine scent of the north woods, I needed something. I needed warmth. I needed reassurance of some kind and the sun was gone so I couldn't get it.

Jude stepped close and wrapped me in his arms and

I was able to relax and forget the chill that had spread through me so quickly, both the physical cooling from an approaching rain storm and the emotional roller coaster that was our new normal. Normal for me, anyway. I wasn't sure about Jude. The man either had the emotions of a chunk of granite or he was very good at hiding his feelings.

His next words said he was a good actor. His voice was hoarse and low as he held me safe. "It'll be okay, Diedre. You'll see."

"What if it's not okay?"

I felt his scowl behind me. "It'll be okay because, if it isn't, I'll make it good. For you. For us."

He lied, of course and I knew it. Neither of us could do anything against the power Lourdes had. I tried not to think about what must be power that was awesome beyond any I could imagine. But Jude's promise made me feel better and soon I was as grounded as Jude, which was much more grounded than I'd been so far, and could turn my attention to the forest. It was so near that, now that I looked closely, I saw a doe and fawn watching us.

I pointed. "The doe and fawn."

"From our dream?"

"Perhaps." We stood that way for a long time watching the pair until they turned and disappeared into the forest and we were left alone beneath the ever darkening sky as lightning flashed and thunder started to rumble.

"We'd best check the pups. They might be afraid." As Jude spoke the words, the first drops fell and we started for the house. By the time we reached the kitchen door, a space of a few yards, we were soaked as those few drops became a torrent that promised to last for hours.

Remembering all the windows in the huge log building that had been open, I looked to locate them from outside so, when we went in, we could find them and close them against the weather. I needn't have bothered. As we watched, they closed themselves. "Of course they do," was Jude's wry comment as we went inside and then to the puppies' room. "How silly of us to think we'd have to do anything at all."

The puppies didn't even know there was a storm. They slept peacefully curled around each other so we left them and headed to our high-end suite of rooms that only had one bedroom and one bed, compliments of Lourdes Jones, the matchmaker who knew a lot about human beings but not the finer points of conventional behavior.

Though, as I examined that huge bed, it occurred to me that it was more likely that of course Lourdes knew unmarried humans didn't normally sleep together but had decided to ignore that piece of information in favor of bypassing some of the more time-consuming elements of courtship in order to short-cut the process.

Whatever his plans were for Jude and me, they seemed to require a loving couple and he was doing everything in his power to mold us accordingly.

CHAPTER 14

Our sleep that night was restless. Of course it was, we were sharing a bed and were afraid we'd be sharing it forever if we accepted his offer of a job. Or until Lourdes Jones decided otherwise. So we started the night as far apart as possible. Somehow, when I woke the next morning, we were curled up together like spoons, my back to Jude's front, with his one arm draped over me and my head pillowed on his other arm.

As soon as we awoke enough to realize we were stuck together like peas in a pod we moved apart and turned towards opposite walls. Jude broke the silence with that sense of humor I was fast learning was a part of him. He said one word. "Oops." I giggled and he continued. "Much longer and Lourdes Jones just might get his wish about us."

If only! But I'd not admit to wishing that. Not in a million years. So instead of replying, I giggled again and the tension disappeared and we took turns in the behemoth of a bathroom. When we were both ready for the day, we worked together to make the bed. "Even though I'm sure there's a trolley around somewhere that would do it for us if we asked it nicely."

"I'd rather do it myself," I replied, shuddering. "That trolley gives me the creeps."

"Me too, but you've got to admit that it's convenient." He aimed his pillow towards the head of the precisely made bedspread. It hit perfectly and he looked to see if I'd noticed his excellent aim. I cheered and he grinned. "Glad you noticed. I am rather good."

"Speaking of that trolley, I'll bet the puppies have been fed and any mess they might have made has been cleaned up so there'll be nothing for us to do in that department." I dropped my pillow beside his and we agreed we'd done an excellent job of making the room presentable. That we worked well together. That we could become a team if we chose to do so. If that was what Lourdes Jones had in mind for us and we chose to accept his offer.

On the way downstairs, lock step with Jude, I thought more about the two of us. How well we worked together and had done so from the very first day. Was it because our personalities complemented each other or was it something special – some kind of alien intervention – that Lourdes had instigated?

No, that wasn't it. I knew the truth. I was fast falling in love with Jude. No, I wasn't falling in love with him. I already was in love and hoped what I felt was authentic instead of implanted by an alien who looked like my uncle. And that love made me super sensitive to him until I was in sync with him and that was why we worked well together.

Which didn't lessen the fact that Lourdes had played us. That thought led to me remembering that last day of the convention. "It was the iced tea that did it. The rat fink."

We were halfway down the stairs. Jude stopped and I almost plowed into him. "He spiked the tea. Of course he did."

"And that somehow made us receptive to the compulsion."

"And to hearing him when he spoke to us mentally."

Lourdes himself appeared as if by magic at the bottom of the stairs. He nodded and half bowed. "You've got me, I'm afraid. Yes, I did add a little something to the iced tea, though even without the additive it was fairly acceptable as tea goes."

"Not compared to the tea you serve here."

He bowed again. "I do like tea. It's one of the delights of Earth and one of the nicer things about living among humans." He tilted his head in thought, then added, "Also Twinkies. I truly like Twinkies. And puppies."

As we reached the bottom of the stairs and came alongside him, he gestured towards the room we'd been in the day before, the yellow, sunshine room, and indicated that we follow him there. "Which is why I ordered both tea and Twinkies for the upcoming visit. I ordered a lot of both."

"Do you mean our visit? Us? Now?"

He didn't answer immediately. Instead, he chose a seat and Jude and I dropped side by side onto the nearby loveseat. The room had contained only chairs the day before and now had a sofa in the only place where we could sit close enough to Lourdes Jones to talk. More matchmaking? The man – alien – had a thing about couples. Human couples. And he was making sure we were attached at the hip.

I looked around for the trolley. It was nowhere to be seen but I was sure it had been there recently, bringing in a sofa to help Lourdes with his matchmaking proclivities.

Now he cleared his throat and answered my earlier question. "The tea and Twinkies aren't only for you two, though you may indulge all you wish, of course." He leaned back and sighed, tired with a weariness that a night's sleep hadn't wiped away. "They are for our upcoming guests."

"Guests?" I looked out the window. All I saw was evergreens and birch trees but I remembered the other buildings scattered throughout the clearing in the forest that was Lourdes Jones' lovely home. "I don't see anyone."

"They aren't here yet." He looked beyond my shoulder to the outside. "Two days from today." He slumped a bit, looking even more weary than when we entered the room. "I'm afraid that, for the first time since coming here, I won't be ready." A sigh came forth. "Which means I'm failing at my job."

He looked defeated instead of like an omnipotent entity. We felt sorry for him, oddly enough. Jude asked, "What about the trolley? It seems to do everything."

Lourdes shook his head. "It does a lot, I'll give you that. But there will be many guests. It's a convention and, as such, will involve many visitors and numerous events. Seminars and such. Not the specific kind of convention where we three met, of course, no dogs involved, but all such gatherings are similar and even the trolley and I working together cannot do all that must be done to have this place ready in time."

He looked straight at us and there was pleading in

his demeanor. "I'm hoping you two will help. I'll greatly appreciate your giving me two days for preparation and three more for the convention itself even if you don't accept my offer when I explain it to you. I'll pay, of course."

What to say? The man was exhausted and ill. "What will be required of us?" Jude's words were carefully chosen.

Lourdes' brightened. "The trolley is self-directed. I simply tell it what to do and it does it, but the other robots must be overseen or who knows what will happen and they do most of the work around here. They must be given orders and monitored to make sure those orders are followed." His voice went low. "So that's it. I'll draw up a list of chores and you two make sure those robots get the place ready in time."

"What is the convention for? It might help for us to know." And what would the attendees look like? Would they have tentacles? Scales? Or would they be like Lourdes and resemble human beings?

"It's informative in nature, as are most conventions." He seemed too tired to say more and we didn't press him.

Lourdes leaned back and watched as the trolley appeared from nowhere as it had the day before except this time instead of tea and snacks, it carried a full, hot breakfast. So conversation was halted as we ate our fill, though I noticed that Lourdes just picked at his food. Because he was ill or because he didn't normally eat human food? As I dug into a hearty breakfast I decided there was much to learn about our host.

When breakfast ended and the trolley disappeared in the direction of the kitchen, Lourdes seemed to gather strength from somewhere inside of himself and continued. "To answer your question about the convention, the galaxy is large and varied, as are its inhabitants. It's wise to occasionally gather together as many different kinds of beings as are willing to attend to work out agreements on how things are to be done. To avoid hostilities and grease the wheels of trade."

"There's trade in the galaxy?"

"Of course. There's commerce everywhere and this place you see around you in this lovely earthly forest is one of the preferred spots for the exchange of information because of its beauty and laid-back atmosphere. And to sell or barter things of interest or value to the galaxy as a whole, of course. Like Twinkies. And tea. And whatever else catches the fancy of our galactic neighbors." He finished with, "So I hold a convention every so often. I scheduled this one before I got sick and there's not time to cancel it. So I hope you will agree to help."

"Of course we will." I turned to Jude because I had no right to speak for him but his brief nod said he, too, would help. When I turned back to Lourdes, I realized he'd followed the exchange between Jude and me and was smiling and there was no way he could have orchestrated Jude's and my agreement. So that was still more proof that not everything happening was preordained by Lourdes and his spiked tea. And that he truly thought we were what he called a bonded pair.

No, more than just a bonded pair. Lourdes saw Jude's and my eyes meeting as validation of his belief that we were a couple in love and being as set as he was on being a matchmaker there was no way I'd dissuade him of that idea so there was no reason to even try. And it was clear that he loved knowing his matchmaking efforts had paid off.

His smile grew until the weariness left his face and he was once more the courtly man who'd opened a door for me. Now he summoned the inestimable trolley with a wave of his hand. "I shall make sure you two also know how to summon it," he said as it appeared. "It comes in handy."

The trolley had a stack of papers on it, two copies of everything we'd need to know to get the place ready for the convention. One for me and one for Jude, plus contracts for each of us to sign. We looked through them with Lourdes available to answer questions but we had none. Either the trolley or Lourdes himself had done an excellent job of describing how to get what was a galactic style luxury resort ready for an influx of beings the appearance of which we couldn't possibly imagine.

The first thing Lourdes did was show us how to summon the trolley. It turned out to be simple, more a way to think than how to wave our hands, though hand waving was involved. We soon learned how to both summon it and tell it what we wanted without talking out loud. Probably the same way Lourdes had mentally communicated with us during our trip north, though when we later tried to talk to each other that way, nothing happened. So it was more complicated than we could imagine. I looked forward to learning more about it.

By the time we could communicate with the trolley and had a grasp of the task ahead, the spurt of energy Lourdes had experienced had dissipated and he left for a nap. "When I truly recover from this bout of illness

I'll once again be myself, but even when that happens if I'm honest I must admit that I'm getting old and I'm sure I'll never regain the level of competence I once had."

He rose and looked out the window at the nearby forest as a small, yellow bird flew past. "I've enjoyed my job here but I find myself more than willing to let two young, healthy, and very nice people who happen to be in love with one another do what I find more and more difficult to do with each passing day."

Neither Jude nor I had the heart to tell him we weren't in love, nor would I admit that he was half right because I was in love with Jude. Not while Jude was in the same room and would hear.

Which raised a question I couldn't help wondering. Could Jude be in love with me? Even a tiny bit? A smidgen? Was it possible? Maybe? Perhaps? Or even just beginning to fall in love?

Probably not.

But the possibility stayed with me far longer than the time it took Lourdes to disappear to wherever he went in the vast reaches of that huge, main building that was both an elegant monument to the intense beauty of the wilderness and a testament to the man we were sure had designed and maintained it for more years than we could imagine. The trees were hundreds of years old. Had they been young when Lourdes bought the place? Had he watched them grow? Or had there been generations of aliens before him?

We set out for one of the outbuildings, the one the trolley said contained the robots that would do the actual work of preparing the place for company. When we found them, lined up in neat rows like toy soldiers, we followed the instructions on one of the pages of notes we'd been given.

Everything we tried worked. We ordered the robots to do a few simple things so we could find out if we could do what Lourdes had requested. If we could turn the buildings and grounds into a fully functioning luxury resort and host a convention unlike any we'd ever attended or even dreamed could exist.

CHAPTER 15

We first tested the robots with something not too difficult, like cutting the grass. Grass was outside so if they screwed up at least the buildings would remain intact. Soon we relaxed because it actually cut the grass instead of mangling the yard or attacking the buildings. When we returned to the main building we found Lourdes sitting on the steps playing with Pete and Repeat. He looked up as we approached and saw his pure love for the two small creatures running around and climbing into his lap every time either was in need of a hug.

I examined the elderly alien and quietly told him, "They are yours."

Lourdes hugged the two puppies. "Thank you." There was something about his demeanor – some subtle thing – that said he'd been waiting for us and playing with the puppies as he waited. We dropped to the steps beside him and waited for whatever would come next because something would. He sighed hugely, knowing we were waiting for him to speak. "I hope I'll be doing the right thing taking these two very sweet beings – puppies -- with me when I return home."

"Home?"

"Yes. Home." He picked up Pete, the white pup with black splotches. "My home planet, that is." After giving Pete a comforting hug he placed him back on the steps and did the same with Repeat, the black pup with white splotches. "We don't have dogs there but I believe they will be comfortable. The gravity and atmosphere are similar and the few differences shouldn't cause problems." He sighed. "Though of course if there are problems I'll bring them back to Earth." He looked from Jude to me. "And hope that you two nice humans will care for them."

"You are leaving?"

He nodded. "I am. I'm ready to retire. To return to my home planet and sit by a lake – yes, we do have lakes and they are similar in many respects to lakes on Earth – and enjoy what time I have left."

"Where is your planet?"

He looked skyward. "Far away. Far, far away. My star is dim. You'd not be able to see it unless you had the most powerful telescope available." He sighed. "It's a lovely planet. Close to our star so our sun fills the sky more than yours does. And the stars are out both day and night because it's a rather dim star." Another sigh. "I miss it. I've enjoyed my time on Earth but I'll be glad to go home."

He looked at us again, slower this time, sizing us up and we somehow knew he was wondering how we'd done with the robots. Our expressions must have said things went well because he nodded briefly. "I can only go home when and if someone takes over for me and agrees to run this place. It was part of the contract I signed all that long time ago." His voice lowered until we could barely hear it. "Which is where you two come in. I hope you will take over. I'm offering you the job."

We were stunned. We didn't know what to say so we said nothing and he seemed to know that humans occasionally – or often – needed time to process new ideas and he was willing to wait while we sorted things out.

"It's why you were called here, you see. Why I went to the service dog convention. To find people to replace me and where better to find such people than at a place where humans who love and work with beings other than themselves congregate." He looked proudly at Jude and me. "And I found two such people." He looked at me. "One person who works with another species on a regular basis."

Then he turned to Jude. "The surprise was a second perfect candidate who pilots crafts somewhat similar to those we use throughout the galaxy." He paused, then added, "You will surely do well with our crafts on necessary trips through the solar system. And beyond. On occasion, that is. Not often, of course, but there are times when such trips are needed." There was something guarded about his face when he said that but he gave no indication what it could be and it was clear he hoped we'd not noticed.

At his mention of space travel Jude stopped breathing. His eyes dilated and I found mine focusing on the man I was in love with. The man who flew jets and now, if Lourdes was to be believed, was being given the opportunity to operate spaceships with technology far beyond anything on Earth.

Jude spoke. "I'm not an astronaut."

Lourdes dismissed his statement. "It's not much different than jets. You know the basics and can learn the rest." His gaze lifted to the blue sky, cloudless and bright. "I suspect you'll love it because most of the pilots I've met do."

"You personally know astronauts?"

"You call them that. They go by many different names throughout the galaxy but all seem to be similar in outlook and abilities and they all pilot craft of one sort or another from one place in the cosmos to a different place for trade and tourism and whatever other reasons beings of all kinds have for traveling between the stars."

Because I was watching Jude so carefully I saw his eyes blaze. Yes, Jude wanted to go into space, to travel from one place to another, to do what no human had done before. And I felt suddenly small and bereft because I wasn't part of that vast universe that was so important to him. I wasn't a part of his dream. My insides heaved and I curled into myself in order not to cry.

Lourdes somehow knew how I felt. His next words were soft with the knowing. "Two humans. Two souls. Together. That's what it must be for the next caretakers." He went silent for a long time, thinking how to express his thoughts. "I've learned a lot about humans during my stay on Earth and the thing I've learned most surely is that they need love and that love seems to be best when it's between one man and one woman. It's the pair bond thing and it's more lovely than I could have ever imagined before seeing it for myself."

He coughed. "So when I began my search for replacements so I could retire, I knew to look for a couple that could both meet the requirements of this particular job and also experience the emotion of love that all humans hope to feel."

He took our hands and placed them together as he'd done at the convention. "I'm so happy I found you two because you fit the requirements perfectly. And so I'm offering you the job. Both of you. Together. As a couple."

My gaze slid away from Jude because I couldn't possibly let him see my thoughts. Not that I knew what those thoughts were because I didn't. I was too confused. I doubted I could have told anyone my name just then let alone how to react to an announcement that could only have come from an entity that knew a lot about human beings while in a way, knew nothing of them at all.

"I hope you two will consider the offer as you help with the upcoming convention and meet beings from all corners of the galaxy. It will give you an idea what the job entails. Part of the job, anyway. The part here in the forest, among these buildings and the surrounding trees and lakes. After our guests are gone, I'll see what can be done to fill you in on the other part. The part that takes place beyond Earth."

I looked at Jude, then, because I wanted to see his reaction to being told he'd soon be in space and I saw that blaze of eagerness as when Lourdes first mentioned space but now it was multiplied a thousand times. He wanted this job and he wanted it badly. But he couldn't have it unless I, too, accepted the offer. Because we'd been offered it as a couple. Even though we weren't.

Lourdes stood up and our joined hands dropped away. He turned from Jude to me. "You, Deidre, were chosen for your love of dogs, which I believe translates to a love of all beings. In two days, when those other beings begin arriving, you'll get a feel for what they are like."

He paused, then continued, as he lifted the two puppies and held them against his elderly face, closing his eyes momentarily at the feel of their soft fur against his skin. "I hope by the time the convention ends you, Diedre, will know how you feel about the job." He then turned to Jude. "And afterwards, when we take a tour of the solar system, I hope you, Jude, will know what you want the answer to be."

I didn't know how I'd feel about alien beings in two days' time but I already knew what Jude wanted. He wanted the space between the planets and, perhaps, between the stars. As we watched Lourdes walk away, I knew that, though I didn't know how I'd feel about aliens I did know one thing. I knew what I wanted more than anything before in my life. I wanted Jude. And Jude wanted space. And he couldn't have it unless I agreed to take the job.

During the next two days, as we learned to direct and monitor the robots and get the place ready for the upcoming convention, we learned more about Lourdes Jones and why he was in a remote place in the wilderness that was north of most the inhabited world.

"Because it's uninhabited, that's why." He sipped the tea he so loved as he explained. "It wouldn't do at all for humans to see vessels of all sorts drop from the sky and then, after a day or so, or a week or two if they are enjoying an extended vacation, lift once more into the heavens." He shook his head. "No, it wouldn't do at all. There would be questions. Investigations. Possibly laws passed against it."

"There are resorts and a town at the south end of the lake," I reminded him.

He agreed. "But those places are far enough away that if the vessels arrive and leave at night, no one is ever the wiser."

"What about noise?"

He tut-tutted. "There are noise ordinances in the galaxy just as there are on Earth. Who'd want loud vehicles with disgusting exhaust to drop by and ruin a perfectly lovely day?" He shook his head. "No one, that's who, so the spaceships that will soon arrive and depart will not bother the residents along the shores of this fair lake. No, the only thing we must concern ourselves with is the possibility of someone seeing them take off or land in the middle of the night. And that's why this place consists of many hundreds of acres of wilderness with only one rude road. For privacy."

I remembered the dreams that had started us on our journey. "Do those spaceships light up the forest when they leave or depart? Is that the light in the forest in our dreams?"

Lourdes nodded. "It is and it's a lovely sight and you must get extra sleep the night before or perhaps a nap the day before they are to arrive so you can stay up all night to greet them and see the lights." The memory of that light in the forest made the whole thing seems less intimidating. It had been lovely and diffuse, like spun silver moonbeams.

The resort was ready for the convention. Then the time came for the aliens to arrive.

Jude and I had taken a nap during the afternoon so we were wide awake and waiting after a filling dinner because, as Lourdes reminded us, we'd have a full night's work ahead of us directing aliens of one type or another to whichever building could best accommodate their needs and particular physiognomies. It was a task best done by us because the robots couldn't be trusted and the trolley couldn't do it all.

We spent the night watching plumes of light descend from the sky and then blink out as one spaceship after another touched the ground so gently there was no shaking of the earth through some kind of alien engineering Jude couldn't wait to discover.

We led beings that for the most part could pass for human in any town if one didn't look too closely to buildings and handed them printouts of the scheduled events for the upcoming convention. Because it was a convention. Everything was complete by the time the night ended and the first faint streaks of dawn told us the arriving was complete because everything had been so well coordinated that it was over with before anyone watching would think anything unusual was going on.

And through it all, Jude's enthusiasm grew and my insides clenched as I wondered if he'd even notice me in his eagerness to learn everything possible about the ships that plied the space between stars. Would he forget about me? Or, if he happened to remember I existed, would I only be a means to an end?

CHAPTER 16

As it turned out, I was wrong about one thing. Yes, Jude was so eager to see and then fly a space ship that he was unable to stand still but, no, he didn't forgotten I existed.

As we saw the last of the space ships drop to earth throughout the night and disappear into what resembled a hill and was actually a very large hanger, we returned to our suite of rooms for a brief nap before taking up the duties of the coming four days, a rest we'd need because we were in charge of a convention and hadn't the faintest idea what to do or how to do it. Four days because the first day was a day of rest for the galaxy-wide travelers before the convention began.

That day was so laid back it hardly existed.

The first day of the convention would be different. Lourdes would be by our sides. The trolley would inconspicuously come behind and mop up after any faux pas we'd make. The wilderness setting would put every being of every species in a good enough mood to overlook minor mistakes. But we were still so nervous neither of us could sleep the night before the big day.

Of course, we were together in that huge, King-sized bed. As far apart as possible, but still beneath the same comforter and almost as uncomfortable as the first night, though by then we'd worked out where each of us would be so we could actually sleep without feeling stupid. But none of that mattered because we were fully awake and unable to even lie still. Because of the convention. The stress and the excitement of it.

"Sorry," Jude muttered as he rolled over for about the hundredth time as the first fingers of dawn showed on the horizon, pulling the blankets off of me and then, after swearing under his breath, giving them back.

"I can't sleep either." I sat up and propped my elbows on my knees and dropped my head onto my hands.

Jude chuckled. As usual. The guy saw humor in everything. "Sharing a bed isn't helping, is it?"

I dropped my hands and sat up straight and was glad for Jude being – Jude. I laughed along with him. "We should be used to it by now. We've slept in shared motel rooms and beds ever since this whole thing began."

"Yep." He sat up too, giving up on trying to sleep. "Want some tea? I can get some."

"Do you suppose Lourdes has coffee?"

"We could use some for a change."

"You'd think there'd be coffee in such a well-stocked kitchen." Though we'd not had any so far because Lourdes dearly loved tea.

Jude tossed off the comforter and stood barefoot in briefs and a tee shirt, his standard night wear. How odd that I knew what he wore to bed while not knowing what he felt like beyond the usual, incidental touch that happens in daily life plus the pretend lovemaking we'd done to chase away the compulsion that we now knew had been Lourdes doing what he did best. Being a nice alien who didn't know enough about humans to know that we shouldn't be together like we were.

As a result of Lourdes mistaken understanding of love, I knew a lot about Jude's anatomy. But I didn't know what his face felt like before he shaved or how his hair would trail beneath my fingers or so many other things about him that I wanted to know. To feel. To experience.

I did know his body was warm because it had kept me warm more than once, and taut, and that his posture was straight and tall without trying because it was his nature and that was how he strode towards the door, all male and in charge even if all he was after was coffee. "I'll check it out and, if I find some, I'll make a pot and bring some back for both of us."

"What if there's no coffee or perhaps not a pot to make it with?"

He snorted. "There's a trolley. I'm sure if those things don't yet exist, the trolley will invent them."

I examined the slowly awakening dawn beyond the window as I waited, elbows on knees as I wondered that the night was so still and peaceful while beings from all over the galaxy slept nearby and waited for the convention to begin. If they slept. I had no way of knowing if aliens slept. Perhaps they were playing cards and we ridiculous humans were the only species that required sleep.

Jude was followed by the trolley when he returned and on it was a coffee pot and everything needed to go with the coffee, plus thick sandwiches. Which was when I realized I was hungry. "This can pass for breakfast."

"We won't have time for breakfast. Might as well eat while we can."

We sat side by side in that huge bed and devoured everything on the trolley, then watched as it rolled away. "Is it laughing at us? I think it is."

"Or spying."

"Why would it spy?"

"Because Lourdes ordered it to."

"Why would he do that?"

"To see if the love thing, the pair bonding he believes is a requirement for his project – us -- is going as planned. Where to better check it out than in the bed we share as a loving couple."

I leaned back and groaned. "Will Lourdes ever figure out we aren't a couple?"

Jude leaned against the headboard on his side of the huge bed and then crossed his feet beneath the comforter and his arms behind his head. "No reason to change his mind about us and love. He thinks he knows all there is to know about humans. But I'm guessing even aliens double check their decisions. So he'll send the trolley to spy on us."

Well, Lourdes did know a few things. He had me figured out, I saw it in his eyes. He knew I was in love with Jude. I didn't know how he knew but he did. Not that it made much difference. It took two humans to make what Lourdes called a pair bond and that would require that Jude feel the same about me and he didn't. So I lied to Jude when I spoke next. "He's wrong about us, of course, thinking we're in love."

"Is he?" Jude's voice was suddenly hoarse and low. I'd never heard him sound like that. His arms came forward, his feet uncrossed, and he turned towards me.

"Is he really wrong?"

"I – I – I don't know what you mean."

Jude examined me. We'd turned on a small lamp while eating but it didn't cast enough light to read his expression beyond that his eyes were bright as starlight. "I mean this."

He leaned across the distance between us and pulled me close and kissed me. Not our first kiss by any means, but the first without an ulterior motive. The first that was just between us and didn't have an entity as a third party.

My breath stopped and my body tingled. Then I turned warm. Then I began to throb as the kiss went on and on and grew deeper and harder until we were flat in bed and tangled in the bedclothes and wrapped around each other and I wondered if we were about to actually, physically become that pair bond Lourdes believed we already were.

Problem was, the black of night was already turning to gray in the east. And then the sky grew lighter still until we could make out the trees beyond the window. And still the kiss continued. I couldn't believe we could learn so much about each other in that brief time. How we felt. How we breathed. How we moved.

But somehow we did and might have learned more given even a bit more time. But by the time day was fully there and we pushed off the comforter and sighed because we had a job to do and we'd better get busy, I happily knew I'd been wrong about Jude. He did know I existed. And more.

Jude said what I was thinking. "Guess Lourdes knew what he was doing when he decided we were suited to one another."

"Or else he used some kind of galactic magic on us."

Jude reached out and ruffled my hair, pulling his fingers through the tangled mess that would take forever to straighten out when we left the bed. "No magic other than the usual kind that's been around since forever. You know how it works. The whole man-woman thing. Me Tarzan, you Jane, and we live happily ever after."

"Except our jungle is closer to the arctic circle than the equator and our trees are evergreens instead of the kind that grow in the tropics."

"And we'll travel in spaceships instead of swinging from vines."

"Of course we will."

Except now I no longer saw those spaceships as competition, but rather as a part of Jude. A facet of his personality. "You can't wait to get your hands on the controls, can you?" I watched to see his reaction and it was exactly as I expected.

He grinned as he headed for the bathroom to clean up and change from a lover into the consummate convention host. "I'm salivating with eagerness to learn how those babies fly." But, before he closed the door and showered, he added, "And you'll love it, too. I promise you will."

That remained to be seen. If Jude was involved I'd give it a try. But flying around the universe in what must be a glorified tin can? It was hard to get excited about that first trip through the solar system.

The convention lasted three days, exactly as the service dog convention had done, but the similarity didn't stop there so I wondered what Lourdes had learned from his visit to an Earthly convention. I hoped a lot because I liked to think that Earth had something to teach the rest of the galaxy even if it was only how to organize a gathering in such a way that attendees left knowing more than when they arrived.

It was a gathering of aliens, I reminded myself as the day passed and I scurried from one room to another in the huge log building that turned out to be mostly large, empty rooms that could be configured many different ways for many different uses. The attendees weren't human, not really, even if most of them sort of resembled humans if you didn't look too closely and I didn't because it would be rude to stare. Probably would be rude. I didn't yet know the ins and outs of galactic manners.

But as I smiled and checked boxes on the worksheet on a clipboard similar to the ones found at any convention, I realized I'd probably someday get a chance to learn about those alien manners. Because it was looking more and more like Jude and I would be accepting Lourdes' offer of a job and not just because Jude wanted to go into space and become a rocket jockey. Because the aliens were interesting and who'd have thought an extremely tall – or very short – or quite round – or whatever shape – alien could be so similar to us. But whatever they were like, they were interesting. Every. Single. One.

The first day was workshops. They discussed the already existing rules of the road for getting around the galaxy without interfering with one another and amended those rules as needed to make for more smooth travel. They decided to leave the barter system in place for acquiring whatever one species wanted from a different species because that was easier than trying to collate all the different currencies that changed in value on a regular basis. Pretty much like on Earth.

They also scheduled future meetings for groups of neighboring planets to get together to hammer out local issues. Local being planets that were merely a few light years apart. I found the concept hard to get used to and so did Jude.

We compared notes at night as we reached for each other in that huge bed that now seemed much larger than necessary and discussed the day's business. Tried to discuss it. Like partners must do in order to coordinate whatever was happening. We failed completely as far as the business aspect of our relationship was concerned but we learned a lot about each other and as far as I was concerned that was the most important thing of all. If Lourdes thought we'd already reached a relationship plateau so could ignore the 'us' thing in order to concentrate on the convention thing, he was sorely mistaken. At night we learned about each other. We didn't learn anything major about galactic conventions.

CHAPTER 17

At the end of the convention, we were the perfect host and hostess. Jude and I stood side by side and waved goodbye to the aliens as they entered their spaceships and departed throughout the night, blasting through thick clouds that portended a storm of epic proportions.

The storm was appreciated by Lourdes who remarked how civilization was encroaching close enough to his extensive property that he feared the time would come when the ships comings and goings would be noticed and he'd have to come up with appropriate counter measures. Or we would, as his replacements.

I turned to Jude as the last ship disappeared into the coming storm. "So what do you think?"

"Aliens are different. Interesting and occasionally weird." He raked a hand through his hair, reminding me that I'd wanted to do that same thing numerous times already and hadn't yet got around to it. I vowed to not forget it tonight when we'd not be burdened with the next day's agenda and whether we'd break some unknown alien custom and set off an intra-galactic war. "But I did have a couple of great conversations with pilots. Learned a little about spaceships."

Lourdes had overheard us and now approached, slowly as per his age and the fact he was still recovering from whatever Earthly bug he'd caught. But there was a spring in his step that I surmised was from both feeling better and the fact that the convention he'd been so concerned about not only was over and done with but had gone off well.

There'd been many compliments, he informed us, because he knew we didn't understand a thing they'd said. The words, yes, with the universal translator, but not the nuances of intra-galactic conversations. But he assured us the time would come when we, too, would know enough about aliens and their civilizations and the subtleties of their makeup that we'd know whether they were satisfied or wanted to throttle us. And we'd grow used to those language implants behind our ears.

The aliens had approved of us, he said, and hoped to meet us again when they next stopped by Earth on whatever errand they happened to be on at the time. The compound was lovely, they'd said, and Earth was a kind of garden of Eden, and they always enjoyed their time here.

As we stood there, though, with the hanger doors still open, Jude looked inside and noticed something. "There's a ship still in the hanger." It had been empty before the aliens arrived. We'd checked it out as part of our getting-ready procedure. "Shouldn't it leave soon?"

The storm was building and would burst over us and soak us thoroughly and the lightning and thunder that could be seen approaching would send us running for safety. But those things might not be enough to disguise a spaceship shooting through the sky once night became morning and people were up and about and the world could be seen even through the storm.

"It's not leaving. Not yet." A small smile played across Lourdes' face. "The ship is still here for a reason, as is the pilot. And a contingent of security types."

"Security types?" The hair on the back of my neck stood up. I'd not been so busy during the convention that I'd not learned that pirates were a problem in the galaxy much as on Earth. One of the workshops had been on just that topic. "Is there a reason for concern?"

Lourdes assured us we needn't worry, that the security contingent was there only because the ship they were assigned to had remained behind so they too, were also here. "I requested that a ship stay so you two can be given a ride through the solar system and perhaps beyond. To give you a feel for what I'm asking of you two. And a taste of what Jude will be doing." Jude made no sound but I knew he was silently cheering. "The pilot is a friend of mine." He nodded to Jude. "He's looking forward to giving you a tutorial on spaceships."

"Will I be allowed to take the controls?" Jude's question was breathless.

"Of course. You must fly enough to see what it's like out there," Lourdes said, no longer trying to hide his enjoyment of Jude's eagerness. "I also believe – in fact, I know – that there's a ship on order for you should you two agree to take the job. Because there are occasions when going somewhere is necessary."

"Then you must also have such a ship." Jude looked again into the hanger. "Though I don't remember seeing one."

"I did have a ship once upon a time. But age and

infirmity have caught up with me and I've decided my time as a pilot is over. As on Earth, age changes everyone. But the ship I flew was an older model. You, of course, will get the most updated version because even the most remote outposts must be defensible."

Defensible? Why'd he use that particular word? I didn't like it. Too warlike.

Jude's next words were chosen carefully. "So even though they are armed, they are here for security purposes only." I was sure he asked because he saw my eyes go wide and my face turn white. And he probably avoided using the word 'pirates' for the same reason as Lourdes nodded agreement and my stomach dropped still lower and something cold curled through me.

Jude was in seventh heaven, but I wondered what we were getting ourselves in for if we accepted. And, of course, we would accept if for no other reason than that was the only way Jude's dream of piloting a space ship could come true. The dream he'd never had until now but that didn't lessen his enthusiasm.

The day was anti-climactic as all days must be for those responsible for any convention. There was the clean-up process, accomplished by the robots and overseen by Jude and myself as we insisted Lourdes rest up and do whatever he wished. Which turned out to be overseeing us as we oversaw the robots.

There was also the paperwork, which was something we'd not thought about until we were sure the compound was physically back to normal. For that was how we'd come to think Lourdes' home. As a compound. Larger than a resort with its outdoor spaces and huge buildings but not as large as a military installation. So compound was the proper term and we were soon introduced to a spacious office where all that paperwork was processed.

Of course, being galactic in nature instead of merely Earthly, the office machines and such were a bit different. Larger and smaller at the same time. Larger in that they processed incomprehensible amounts of data in micro-seconds. Smaller in that they took up very little space.

That left most of the office open for comfortable furniture with large windows overlooking the ever-present scenery as whomever was working fed mega blocks of information into the machines and enjoyed the ever-present tea while waiting for it to spit out results. As a bookkeeper, I was impressed and eager to learn more, just as Jude was eager to learn how to pilot a spaceship.

Yes, I realized as I examined the small-yet-large office and thought of Jude piloting a spaceship, when Lourdes chose us, he chose well. Two people with the qualifications required for the job and who, as far as he could tell at the time, were attracted to one another, even though he wasn't human and therefore couldn't correctly quantify the human emotion of romantic love and so hadn't got that part quite right.

We finished up in the office and Lourdes pressed 'send' to inform whatever galactic main office he worked for of the details of the convention.

Then Lourdes did disappear and we knew he was finally resting, most likely gazing out a window in his own quarters, wherever in the huge building they were, and dozing now and then as his elderly body recovered from the stress of the convention and regained that sparking energy that had first brought him to my attention at the service dog convention.

He joined us for dinner but didn't stay long, begging off by saying he'd decided on an early night. We watched him go and then finished our own meal and were glad for the trolley that cleaned up after us so we had nothing to do beyond relax for the rest of the evening before heading to bed ourselves in that multi room suite that contained only one bedroom and one very large bed.

By then we'd worked out a routine. We took turns getting ready for the night in that huge bathroom and climbed onto opposite sides of the bed, carefully remaining as far away from each other as possible. Because we were, after all, not a couple. Not really. And not in love, at least Jude wasn't and I'd not tell him I was more and more in love with him each and every day. No way. I'd keep my dignity.

Each night, though, the distance between us grew less as we tossed and turned in that huge bed. And there was the kissing we'd begun as a protest against the compulsion and continued because we liked it. We always sedately separated to sleep, however, and then inevitably ended up so close together when we woke in the morning that we were wrapped around and entangled with each other so tightly an onlooker couldn't have said where one of us ended and the other began.

When we discussed it like rational adults we said the reason was proximity and not emotion. One bed was the way things were because we couldn't have what we wanted, which would be separate bedrooms and since we were two practical beings who just happened to be in the same bed at the same time and since we were enlightened and not prudes, well, we were okay with whatever happened. Like finding ourselves wrapped in the bedding like Christmas gifts.

That night, though, there was a difference. It began with Jude's sigh on the other side of the bed, followed by a cryptic comment. "The convention is over, thank goodness."

The words were followed by a slight movement, hardly noticeable except I was so sensitive to anything and everything about Jude that he might as well have jumped up and down. What he'd actually done was move infinitesimally closer to me. I was sure of it.

I rolled onto my side, facing him and waited for – something, as I replied. "Yes, and I believe Lourdes was speaking the truth when he said it went well."

Other nights, we'd moved closer only briefly and mostly while asleep and totally unaware of what we were doing and had found ourselves all tangled up together only when waking during the night or in the morning. But we were wide awake now.

I felt rather than saw him rise onto one elbow and wondered if he was looking at me. Or looking for me because it was too dark to make out anything enough to know what it was. "I've been thinking –"

I wanted to move closer but didn't. The dignity thing, again. No way would he know how badly I wanted to touch him, to rake my fingers through his hair, and how had I thought I'd accomplish that earlier when I'd decided to do it next time we were together? Like right now. Because there was no reason to do it that I could justify. I swore silently in pure frustration. But my voice was smooth. "What have you been thinking?"

"About us."

Uh oh.

I thought carefully before replying because his statement could come from several places. It could be romantic, though it probably wasn't. Or about returning home now that we had that option. Or it could be about accepting the business partnership we'd been offered.

I decided the last was the most likely of the three possibilities. That he wanted us to take the job so he could pilot a spaceship. I hoped my voice was businesslike. It probably wasn't. "What, exactly, were you thinking about us?"

"Uh —" He started to say something, then stopped. Then he moved a bit closer still and my breath stopped and my skin started to tingle and there was no way I could stop it. Which meant I was pathetic and couldn't possibly spend the rest of my working life this close to him while being chaste and considerate. No way.

But neither did I want to spend my life away from him if I had the option of being near him. He cleared his throat because he was unexpectedly hoarse. "I've been thinking about Lourdes having chosen us because we are the right people for the job."

There was a pause, then he added, in a totally different tone of voice, one that was hoarse and a couple octaves lower than usual. "No, not just the right people. We are the right *couple* for the job."

CHAPTER 18

This talk was to be about Jude and spaceships. His dream. My guess had been right. "Don't worry, Jude. I won't do anything to jeopardize your chance to be a space jockey. I know how important it is to you."

He moved closer, until he was in the middle of the bed. He reached for me, pulling me towards him which was saying something with the comforter getting in the way. This discussion must be important if we had to be that close that he was willing to go to so much work to get me in the right mood.

Then he confused me totally by asking, "Spaceships? Who said anything about spaceships? Whatever are you talking about?"

I burrowed through the comforter and scooted as close as possible without climbing on top of him because I wanted to be sure he understood what I was about to say even though he'd been the one to initiate the conversation. "I'm talking about the job, Jude. Telling Lourdes we'll take the job so you can fly spaceships. Isn't that what you're talking about?"

Even inches away I could feel the heat radiating from his body. It was a Jude thing. Or a guy thing. I didn't know that many guys to know which. So close to him, though, I could feel both his body heat and his confusion.

I could sense him searching through what I'd said until he figured out what I was talking about. "It's true, I guess, that the job and what I was thinking are all both kind of the same thing. But the part I was talking about wasn't the job part. It was the 'us' part. Just us."

He touched me. Just touched me and I turned to Jello and could only hope to be able to continue to speak rationally while knowing it would be impossible in another few seconds just because that slightly hoarse baritone did things to me. No, not just because of his voice. I'd be Jello even if he was silent if he came even a fraction of an inch closer and that very male heat penetrated my core. But I tried to be casual. "What about us?"

"Us. Just us. Forget the job for a moment and think about us because we are in this thing together. Yes, it would be nice to fly spaceships. But if that's not what you want, then it's not what I want either."

"Really?" It was all I could think to say because that was the last thing I expected of him. Since seeing that first one drop from the sky before the convention began, spaceships were at the top of his life list.

But he wasn't finished. "I'm talking about you. Me. Us. And the future."

"What future?"

"Our future."

"Do we have a future?"

"That's what I'm asking. Do we?"

"I don't know."

"Then think about it. Please. Think about us and all the years ahead."

I went quiet. "What about those years? What do you want me to consider? To see? To look for in that future?"

He came still closer until our bodies were aligned and touching, leg to leg, thigh to thigh, with only enough space between our upper bodies to be able to breathe. "I want you to see us together. To think if we can be together. To decide if you want that for us."

"It's what Lourdes wants. Is that what this is about? Lourdes?"

"Lourdes is an interesting alien, I'll give you that, and it would be fantastic to fly through the solar system and beyond, but, no, this isn't about him and the job. It's about us. Us. Forget spaceships and aliens and all of the rest and, instead, think about us. Just us. Together. For the rest of our lives." A pause, then, "Can you picture that?"

Of course I could! I'd been doing not much else for days. But my words were as smooth as silk when I said, "I can." Followed by, "Why now? This is out of left field and I'm trying to come to grips with it. So I need to know what you aren't saying as much as I want to know what you are. What's the rest of your question?"

Another pause, this time on his part. "The rest is that I love you and want to marry you. If you want to, that is, and I know this is a totally awkward place to ask and a completely awkward way to ask it, but I'm tired of waiting and I'm also tired of sleeping in the same bed with you and wishing we were married so it would be where we both wanted to be instead of where Lourdes put us. So forget the place and the very awkward situation we find ourselves in. I'm asking you to marry me."

"Okay." It was amazing that I could speak. I wasn't sure I could until I tried it and then just the one word. I hoped it was enough.

"Okay? What does that mean?"

One word wasn't enough. He needed more. "It means, it's all okay, the whole thing, even the Lourdes job offer, and of course I'll marry you whether we take the job or not."

He must have been holding his breath because it all rushed out in a big whoosh as I felt his body relax beside mine and then that tiny distance between us disappeared and I learned that the kisses and incidental touching so far had just been practice and by the time we finally fell asleep, still wrapped around one another, we both knew what the future would hold. Us.

We didn't discuss Lourdes and his offer of a job because that was the furthest thing from our minds and the least important. It had been what got us together but it wasn't what was keeping us that way.

But as morning came, bright and clean after the downpour that had masked the leave taking of the aliens we agreed that when we saw him next we'd tell Lourdes we'd take him up on his offer.

We met him as we came downstairs and followed him into the bright yellow room for another relaxed breakfast. He smiled the Lourdes smile we'd come to recognize as his signature expression and said he was glad we'd decided to take the job.

He already knew and that made Jude pissed. "How do you know?" He glared at Lourdes. "Are you reading our minds? Because if you are, we'd appreciate it if you'd stop."

Lourdes just continued smiling that blinding smile.

"Not at all." It went up a few watts if such was possible. "I took one look at you two this morning and knew everything was perfect." He considered us, top to bottom, side to side. Both of us together. "Though that look you both are wearing now and weren't until this morning tells me that I've just learned something about humans that I didn't know before. Even though I thought I did."

We speared him with looks because in spite of what he said surely he was reading our minds. How else would he know what had transpired during the night? "What have you learned?"

"That I didn't know as much about human mating rituals as I thought I did, and I truly thought I was an expert after reading much and watching many movies and TV and so on."

He patted us on the shoulders and indicated we take the only sofa in the room as he took the seat opposite, just as we'd done days earlier. "But from the looks on your faces this morning and the fact that you are both absolutely glowing, I see I was wrong about many things.

"Much has happened since that service dog convention where I believed you'd become a bonded pair. I truly thought it had happened there. But your relationship has changed daily since then and last night seems to have brought it to its logical conclusion. A conclusion I thought had already been achieved. But I was clearly wrong."

He added, as an afterthought, "And that's how I knew you were going to take the job. Not because I read your minds, because that would be rude, but because it was obvious as you came down the stairs that you were about to agree to both the job and a life together and I'm so glad you've made both decisions.

"Because you have obviously figured out the pair bonding thing for yourselves even though I thought I'd done it for you." He sighed and added, "When I return home, I'm going to do further research into the mating habits of humans. Obviously they are more complex than I realized."

Jude coughed and Lourdes' look said he knew Jude had more to say. That he, Lourdes, hadn't covered everything. That there was more, though he couldn't imagine what it could be. Jude said, "We'd like to get married."

Lourdes flushed. "Of course. That's what humans do and how foolish of me to forget even a minor thing like marriage. The mating ritual."

Jude continued. "That means a marriage license and a waiting period, then either a pastor or an official of some kinds. And two witnesses."

"Because that's how it's done on Earth." Lourdes nodded thoughtfully. "I assume you can manage those things in the nearby town?"

I spoke up as something occurred to me. "Can we get married here? In the compound?"

Lourdes covered his surprise well. "I'm sure it can be arranged." He peered out the window. "I believe the spaceship pilot can be one witness and I can be the other." He wasn't sure about the rituals surrounding human pair bonding. "Should the security forces be involved or should they stay away?"

"If they look human then they can do whatever they choose." I added, "It's traditional to have a small celebration after the ceremony and they might be interested in that whether they attend the ceremony or not."

"A party?"

"Similar."

Lourdes nodded. "I believe they'll like that. I've never met a military contingent of any species that didn't enjoy a good party."

Jude cleared his throat. "All of which is to be done after we take that promised trip through space." He looked at me apologetically. "There's a waiting period before getting married. No sense wasting those days if they can be put to good use." The man was truly obsessed with flying. "I'm sure both the spaceship and the security force have things to do and places they should be so every day counts." Yes, he definitely was obsessed with all kinds of craft that could defy gravity. And with space. And probably many other things I'd learn about over time.

We got a marriage license that very day and returned to the compound where we met the security force and I was introduced to the pilot of the spaceship whom Jude already knew. They bumped fists as we climbed aboard the ship that night as soon as it was dark enough for Lourdes to decide we'd not be noticed by the inhabitants of the town on the south side of the lake.

And, without me knowing it was happening because the ship had some kind of artificial gravity – or a dampening field – or something else I probably couldn't imagine – we were in the air and then, after what seemed mere moments, I looked out a view port at the blackness of space and at Earth receding as we flew fast and then faster still towards some point I couldn't see.

The security types were in the back because they were using the trip to hone their skills. They planned on doing so when Jude took over the controls. They believed it would be good practice for when things went wrong because of course he'd mess up and the resulting chaos would be similar to what would happen if the ship had been damaged by enemy fire. They'd figure how to compensate. Good practice for the real thing.

About that they were wrong. Jude piloted the ship as if he'd been flying spaceships all his life and the actual pilot, someone whose name I couldn't pronounce so was told to call him Sam because it was as close as we could come to what it really was, said he'd be proud to have Jude as a copilot and would recommend him for full pilot status as soon as we returned to Earth.

Soon he and Jude were best buddies as they discussed the finer points of space and ships and a million other things I didn't care about. So I left the cockpit, if that's what it was, to explore the parts of the ship I was allowed to visit. Not where the security forces were because that part included tactical gear I couldn't imagine but might accidentally activate and blow us all to smithereens. Not to mention that I didn't know them and they didn't know me so the possibility of one or the other of us making an intra-galactic faux pas was real. So I found what must be a viewing room, with windows through which space showed and went on seemingly forever.

The view beyond the view port was interesting. Black, yes, but filled with dots I wish I recognized but didn't. Occasional glimpses of planets. Earth? Mars?

The rest of the solar system planets? They were round and floated in space and that was all I knew except, when we passed Earth again, it was blue and I almost cried at how beautiful it was. Blue and bright in all that blackness.

CHAPTER 19

As I gazed out that viewing port, I saw a dot that wasn't a planet or a star. It was something else and it was coming towards us. I watched as it grew until it became another spaceship and black as the black of space with no markings to identify it. The ships from the convention had been all kinds of bright colors with hieroglyphs telling where they were from and who they represented. This one was different.

As I watched, still another ship blinked into existence from a different direction and quite far away as distance was measured in space but coming closer with each passing second. Two spaceships? Interesting.

Then a klaxon went off and my insides threatened to come up because the klaxon emergency call is universal. Its scream was so loud it disrupted every cell in my body and set me vibrating to its call. Then red lights began blinking furiously. Those lights screamed danger. Again, red lights must be universal and the ships heading our way were surely the reason. My stomach rebelled still more and my heart almost stopped.

I should do something. React some way. But I didn't know what to do. I was alone in the viewing room and there'd been no introductory speech telling passengers what to do in an emergency so I was frozen to the spot, able only to stare out the viewport as those ships closed in, one almost ready to dock with us and the other still far away but closing in fast.

Pirates. They must be pirates. I'd read about Blackbeard so I knew the black ship already deploying a boarding tunnel was intentionally black so as to be invisible until it chose to make its presence known. Now it was making its move. Connecting to our ship. Quickly snaking the tunnel towards us. It would rob us. Then what?

The doorway to the viewing room burst open and one of the security types ran in. "Come. Now." He said no more, just grabbed my arm and dragged me after him with one hand while the other carried a weapon of some type. It was large and dangerous looking but would it be effective? What weapons did the pirates have?

I got my feet under me and ran with him. Soon we were in the control room where Jude, Lourdes and the pilot were furiously working controls as the security type in charge of me thrust me into a person-sized cubicle and slammed the door shut. Then he – or it – ran out of the control room still at top speed, never having stopped or even slowed down since bursting into the viewing room, presumedly to rejoin his companions and repel the pirates who by then surely had that boarding tunnel secure against our ship.

I felt the sides of the cubicle. Was it a life pod? If the ship was destroyed would I be ejected into space to float forever between planets?

It had a window so I could see what was happening

even though there seemed to be nothing I could do to change my status. No way to get out, no controls, no handle with which to open the door. Just the window through which to watch while others either overcame the pirates or died horrible deaths.

I'd undoubtedly been thrown into the pod to get me out of the way so everyone else could concentrate on repelling the pirates instead of worrying about me. So, since there was nothing else I could do no matter how I tried, I simply watched. And cried. And wondered how I'd ended up in a spaceship somewhere between planets that was being attacked by pirates. I also prayed. Fervently.

I watched Jude, the pilot, and Lourdes work those controls, taking evasive action to pull away from the pirates. To prevent that boarding tube from connecting. To prevent them from boarding.

The control room had windows all around, giving a three hundred sixty degree view of space. I could see the pirates trying to connect the boarding tube. I also saw the second ship arrive, the one that had come from far away. I wanted to scream to those in the control room that more pirates were coming and they'd have to deal with them also. If they could.

Did they know the second ship was there? Did they see it? It wasn't black so was easy to notice. It was blazing white with black logos.

As I stared I realized it kind of resembled the old-fashioned police cars, only it was larger. And as I regained some of my ability to think, I realized it wasn't matte black like the pirate ship. It wasn't trying to hide. So was it here to help?

It wasn't targeting our ship. In fact, it zoomed past

us and headed for the pirate ship. Soon its own docking tunnel shot towards the dull black ship. Grabbed it. And connected. But the pirates had succeeded in boarding our ship.

Even in my pod I heard them. They were in the hall and heading towards the control room. As I watched helplessly a contingent of ragged looking individuals poured into the control room, carrying weapons straight out of a comic book. But they were followed by our security types with their own weapons and they were coming as fast as they could run.

A fight followed. Light flashed from those science fiction weapons as Jude and the others flying the ship worked furiously to keep us on course as the security types fought off pirates intent on taking over. The intensity of the battle increased. It was impossible to know which side was winning.

Then, as I watched with my face pressed against the window in the pod, the tide of battle shifted and I could make out individual fights as the general melee turned into small battles throughout the room.

The pirates had exploded into the control room with confidence and superior numbers. But the security types were professionals who fought with the discipline and expertise found only in well trained and experienced military units. As I watched I noticed their expressions, or lack of expressions. They were doing a job without emotion, without fear. Because they'd done this before? Because it was routine?

Sooner than I'd have thought possible those security types were once more in charge of our ship. The small fights ended as first one and then another group of professionals overcame the pirates.

Then there was no more fighting. The pirates were herded into a group against a wall with their hands behind their backs.

Security dragged the pirates out of the control room. I wondered if there was a prison on the ship and decided such places might be found on all spaceships if pirates were a problem. And evidently they were.

Beyond that three hundred sixty degree window I watched as the late arrival, the white ship, sent a humongous net over the pirate ship. Soon the boarding tunnel between the pirate ship and ours was disengaged and the white ship towed the pirate ship away from us and we floated free, our engines shut off as were the engines of the other two vessels. And we all three drifted through space.

Jude opened my pod and pulled me into his arms and just held me without speaking and I never wanted him to let go. Everything, the attack, the fight, and the victory, had happened so fast that my body hadn't yet caught up and I was shaking uncontrollably. I looked at him and said, "I thought you were going to die."

He laughed. Laughed! "Not even close. And no fatalities. As usual, I'm told." He saw my expression. Terror. Panic. "Pirates aren't greedy enough to put their lives at risk. Not worth it and I knew that because I was briefed before I was allowed on board so I'd know what to do if the worst happened. And it did." He thought a second. "So I'll know in the future that pirates aren't as brave as in the comic books." I almost barfed. Again.

But he still held me, knowing I needed it, that my fear still lingered even as his dissipated in the euphoric aftermath that was gripping everyone except me. Jude, Lourdes, the pilot and the two security types still there while the rest had disappeared with the captive pirates. All of them, every single one of them except me was high-fiving everyone else and dancing among the controls.

They were insane, all of them, including Jude.

Except, as I watched them slowly come down from their high, I accepted that the high they were experiencing was probably necessary, a release from the tension of battle. It was a military thing and possibly an essential part of getting past what had happened and so perhaps it was okay.

They probably deserved every second of their celebration. They'd protected the ship, its contents, and me. So I watched without feeling critical even though I didn't share their euphoria. I was simply glad to be alive and glad I still had Jude.

The white ship came close and another boarding tunnel appeared and connected with our ship and soon beings from that white behemoth were in the control room and, yes, they were police of a galactic sort and were there to get the paperwork done that went with capturing a band of space pirates so the owner of our ship could be properly compensated for whatever damage had been done and the pirates could be punished.

It was exactly how things were done on Earth when pirates stole from honest merchants and were caught. The galaxy might be larger than Earth but many things were the same. That knowledge gave me a feeling of security nothing else could and I felt better and better as the minutes passed and everyone acted as if what had happened was routine and I began to put behind me the fact that I'd expected to be killed.

Because I hadn't been. We'd all survived and were doing just fine and Jude was in his element surrounded by testosterone and military types while doing his new favorite thing -- flying a ship through space. I tried to make myself invisible as I accepted that this was to be my life from now on. Spaceships. Aliens. And occasional pirates. I acknowledged that there's no such thing as a perfect society, not on Earth, not in space, not anywhere in the galaxy.

The universal translator meant I understood what everyone was saying as they went through the legal processes involved with the situation, taking care to explain everything minutely for Jude's sake because he was new but would most likely be involved in other such events in the future because, as Lourdes explained to everyone there, we'd shortly be taking over his job and so would become part of the galactic force protecting Earth and providing passing aliens with a safe and comfortable place to stay and rest for a bit while on whatever journey they were on.

Then we continued our trip through the solar system as if nothing had happened. As if the pirate attack was a minor interruption in an otherwise pleasant excursion.

Were pirate attacks so common they didn't make a ripple on the smooth surface of galactic life? Would Jude have to deal with them often or were they rare events? Would I always wait and wonder if he'd return alive?

Someone turned to me. I was the added element in the equation and should be given comfort. I could see the thought in the not quiet human eyes of the security type assigned to take care of me. To take care of the civilians.

I was told such attacks were not common. The pirates had targeted us because of the convention. They'd figured there must be treasures to be had from such a galaxy-wide event and chose the last ship because there'd be no other ships to come to its aid. Or so they thought. They'd not counted on the galactic police being on standby. That made me feel better. Slightly.

I'd have to deal with things like this in the future. This must be what military spouses dealt with every day of their lives. If they could live with it, so could I.

What else would I have to deal with in the future I'd never in my wildest dreams expected and yet wanted badly because it included Jude? What would Jude and I face as the years passed? My mind went blank and all I could think was that I'd find out, one experience at a time.

I concentrated on the introductory trip we were on. The trip through the solar system and beyond, into outer space. The space between the stars.

We circled planets and cruised through the asteroid belt and admired the rings of Saturn and then went into what was I decided must be overdrive for a spaceship. We passed through the Kuiper belt at the farthest reach of the solar system without me knowing it because the asteroids were so far apart they weren't easily visible.

And still we flew, on and on and into the void of space itself. As the ship moved smoothly through that black emptiness with Jude at the controls and loving every minute of it, I decided time would tell what my new life would be like. It would work itself out.

I returned to that viewing room where I stood alone

because everyone else on the ship had a job to do. I was the single passenger. I took in the wonder of the universe, all black and boring at times and full of color and life at other times and I knew that the years ahead would not only be ones of Jude and love, they would also be very, very interesting.

But, I decided that for the most part I'd stay on Earth.

CHAPTER 20

We already had the marriage license thanks to that earlier trip to town. All we needed was to find someone to officiate and then figure out just where on the extensive grounds of the compound we should have the ceremony itself and what the celebration afterwards should be like. Similar to ones on Earth that involved humans? Or was there some other kind that would be more appropriate for the guests at this particular ceremony who might look human but weren't?

We finally decided that since we'd invite the pastor performing the ceremony and his family to partake of the celebration afterwards because that was usual in such situations, at least on Earth, we should probably not shock him too much with some kind of alien party. So it would be an Earthly type wedding followed by an equally earth-like reception.

Besides, we didn't know how beings in other parts of the galaxy celebrated marriages so didn't know how to do anything different. Or if other worlds even had marriage. But earthlings did.

Earthlings. Who'd have thought I'd ever casually use that word in my everyday life?

Thankfully, Lourdes was sure the aliens were

humanish enough to pass muster with anyone who didn't get too close or mingle with them for too long and after years working in foreign places – meaning planets other than their own – they were experts at keeping an imperceptible distance from their hosts and blending in. And they could eat human food, though if there were a few alien tidbits in another room they'd appreciate the thoughtfulness.

So ultimately, the result was a normal Earth wedding between two humans, the kind in which the liquor was far enough away from the main event that those who wanted to imbibe wouldn't ruin the reception for those who didn't drink. The fact that it wasn't liquor but instead was some kind of alien treat wasn't important. Whatever it was would probably involve a few guests who got carried away and managed to insult everyone within earshot. Of course it would. It was a wedding.

We hoped the pastor wouldn't notice a few oddities in the guests. Like extra digits. Or pointy ears. If he thought the unusual hair colors were the result of hair dye, we wouldn't tell him otherwise and we spent a fair amount of time arranging the seating so the aliens would be far enough from the pastor that he'd not notice a few irregularities.

Then we turned our attention to what to wear and were soon so concerned over the matter of clothes that we forgot about the aliens. I found a lovely dress online but it would take forever for it to be shipped and the security forces were on a schedule. If we wanted them to attend we couldn't wait and we were counting on the ship's captain to be a second witness so time was of the essence.

A tux for Jude from the nearby town that rented tuxes for graduations would be a bit over the top for a small, informal wedding but where could we find the right casual but still formal suit? Again, we found one online but shipping would be too slow and though Jude insisted his usual jeans would be fine, I didn't believe they would go with the lovely, long, formal dress I truly wanted and had pictured ever since I was a little girl playing dress-up. The exact one that I saw online and couldn't figure out how to get in time.

The answer was the trolley. Lourdes was surprised and slightly disappointed that we didn't think of it ourselves. "You're going to be in charge here. You must learn to utilize all available resources and the trolley is one of the best." He smiled that thousand watt smile that was growing stronger by the day as he recovered physically and let one stressor after another disappear because soon he'd be leaving everything to us. "You'll have your wedding attire and you'll have it in time. Is there anything else you need to make the day complete?"

Shamefaced, he added, "I should have realized human pair bonding requires a ceremony because all things humans do seem to require appropriate ceremonies and that ceremonies require the proper accoutrements. How foolish of me. I must do more thorough research next time."

So one beautiful summer day after the trolley presented us with clothes that were perfect – of course – and Lourdes and the trolley together cooperated on getting everything else ready because, as the engaged couple we shouldn't have to do anything at all – and the middle aged pastor from a small church in the nearby town we'd enlisted for the actual ceremony arrived right on time -- we got married.

It took place in that huge room with the stone fireplace. The setting impressed the pastor. He'd not realized such a nice resort existed in the area. His wife and three daughters enjoyed everything and said they'd be happy to recommend this resort to anyone looking for a place to stay.

As politely as possible, hiding the panic his words invoked, we asked them not to do that. We explained that we were always overbooked and wouldn't be able to accommodate any more guests. They said they totally understood and wouldn't even mention we existed. We were grateful and relieved.

The wedding itself was short and lovely, as all weddings should be, and the reception went well. The pastor and his family thought our guests were polite if a bit reclusive. We explained that they were foreigners and the pastor agreed that must be the reason for their reticence and didn't attempt to get too close so as not to make them uncomfortable, another thing we were grateful for.

Every so often the guests -- the security types -- would disappear one at a time to another room. The pastor noticed but pretended not to. That's the way weddings worked, he whispered, and added that possibly their home country believed in alcohol more than he did and that was fine with him.

The day finally came to a close. The pastor and his family departed. The security types retreated to their quarters to finish off their special treats, walking unsteadily and helping each other along.

Jude and I changed into the outdoor clothes we had

waiting, grabbed the camping gear that was already packed, and headed for our brief honeymoon along the shore of the large, spider-shaped lake we'd driven along to find the compound and Lourdes.

We were looking for a specific place. If we could find it. We wanted to see for ourselves the limpid waters of our dreams and the tiny, white beach fronting a huge forest where a doe and fawn came to drink at dusk and where, when full dark arrived, a mysterious light appeared somewhere among the trees.

We found the beach with hardly any trouble at all. It was the only beach anywhere near the compound. We took off our clothes for the swimsuits beneath and jumped into that lake. We expected warm, comfortable water. We almost froze to death until our bodies grew used to the cold water of all northern lakes. We didn't swim as long as we might have if the water was warmer, but that was okay because the birchbark canoe of our dreams that was available for Lourdes' galactic guests was pulled up on the shore. It took us in and out of coves and creeks that were fingers along the shore and was as good as floating on the lake would have been if the water had been warmer.

That night, before retiring to the two person tent we'd set up between the beach and the forest, we leaned back and wondered if we'd see the light in the forest that had been a part of our dreams. It had been in some of them but not all.

We knew what it would look like. It would be a diffused, white glow that lit up the sky but didn't overpower it because the stars could still be seen everywhere in the sky except where it glowed.

We were about to give up when it appeared. White

and pure and not accompanied by a sound of any kind. We watched as it shone through the trees and grew to a large, glowing ball, and then rose into the heavens.

It was so beautiful I almost cried as, beside me, Jude laughed so hard tears ran down his cheeks and he slapped his hands on his thighs. "It's the spaceship I piloted. The one we went for a ride in. The security force is leaving. Glad they could stay for the wedding." He saluted it lazily.

"There will be another such light in the sky when the ship I'm getting arrives, plus an additional glow for the companion ship that will carry the pilot back home. Lourdes will be on that one as a passenger."

"Because he'll be going home."

"Wherever his home is."

We examined the stars scattered across the sky and couldn't even begin to guess which was Lourdes' home star, if we could even see it, which he'd said we couldn't because it was dim. We wished we could locate it so we could think about him and know he was happy.

There were millions of stars not visible to our eyes in addition to the ones we could see. We pretended we knew where in the galaxy Lourdes would live out his remaining days. We wished him well.

"I hope his home planet can handle two puppies."

"Puppies are cute. Anyone – any species – anywhere in the galaxy -- is sure to love them."

"I suspect we'll get our own puppies one of these days when another kid will be looking for homes for whatever puppies will be available."

"We'll have to go to town every so often to find them."

As the spaceship disappeared and the white light dimmed and then winked out we turned back to the tiny beach and there, just as in our dreams, we watched a doe and fawn drink for a moment before retreating into the forest. But this was reality with sounds and scents and the love of a mother for her child and was a thousand times better than any dream.

Then we put deer and puppies and aliens and incredible trolleys and pirates and everything else out of our minds and headed for the tent so we could concentrate on becoming what Lourdes had always thought we were. A bonded pair.

We hadn't become that bonded couple in exactly the way he'd thought, at the convention when he'd played matchmaker. But when we crawled into that tent we were definitely two people deeply in love.

THE END

Hi,

I'm Florence Witkop and I hope you enjoyed *Come With Me.*

To leave a review, click on the link beneath the *Come With Me* cover on my author's website http://www.FlorenceWitkop.com and you'll be directed to the Amazon page where reviews can be posted. I hope you will do so because reviews, while not necessarily the deciding factor in sales, are nice to have and I enjoy reading every single one.

If you want to see what else I've written, while you're there check out the other books on the website. Again, it's http://www.FlorenceWitkop.com

My next book is titled *Keeping Susanna Safe* and has all the elements every good, satisfying love story should have. Hero. Heroine. Situation they must deal with. Plus a heaping helping of love because love makes the world go round and, in my opinion, should be included in every good story, not just romances. As in all of my books, my characters are normal, well-adjusted people thrust into abnormal situations and the story is how they get through those situations and fall in love in the process.
Keeping Susanna Safe has no sci/fi or paranormal elements. Instead, there are good guys and bad guys in black hoodies and of course the good guys win. It's set in a small town – actually a tiny hamlet so small you can find a building just by standing in the middle of

town and looking around. And, of course, the inhabitants are characters in the book.

If you want to know what it's about, here's the back cover description:

Nature is out to kill her. So is the cartel.

Susanna rents a cottage in a tiny town beside a trout stream where she can lick her wounds after quitting a dead-end job. Royce, a laid-back, small-town businessman who schedules work around when the fish are biting helps the pretty newcomer learn how small towns operate.

Then strangers in black cars with tinted windows show up looking for Susanna. She doesn't know why they are interested in her but Royce doesn't like the vibes they give off and vows to protect the woman he's coming to love.

He soon finds himself up against men in black hoodies with murder on their minds as thunderstorms, tornadoes, and a flood threaten Susanna's flimsy cottage -- with her inside.

Royce is just a small-town businessman who likes fly fishing and Susanna. Can he keep her safe when both the cartel and the weather are doing their utmost to end her life?

And here's the beginning of *Keeping Susanna Safe*:

Chapter 1

I had a place to go. A summer rental. I'd made a deposit and signed a lease. So with the key in my purse I did what I'd been planning to do since being passed over for promotions so many times I'd gotten sick of being invisible.

I quit.

My bosses weren't happy.

"Are you sure this is what you want?" There was an undercurrent in the room as they read and then re-read my resignation. They'd not paid any attention to me while I was employed so why the exit interview?

I'd answered politely. "Yes it's what I want."

The unreadable faces of the men across the table let the silence drag on forever until finally one of them asked, "Why are you quitting?"

Again, I answered politely. "Because I wish to pursue other opportunities."

They looked at one another and then back at me and something about their expressions sent a shiver through me as one of them, it didn't matter which because they were clones of each other, spoke in a voice that was meant to be placating and wasn't. "You'll stick by the non-disclosure agreement you signed when you were hired."

I was a lowly clerk. The possibility of my knowing company secrets was so ridiculous I almost laughed. "Of course I will."

But they continued to stare at me and mentally take me apart until I got so tired of playing nice that I added to my answer in the most scathing tone of voice I could manage. "Besides, the NDA is only important if you break the law." I was so tired of their superior attitude that I spit out my next words. "And you don't do that, do you? You don't break the law." Then I stared at them and folded my arms across my chest as I dared them to respond.

They continued to look at me with no expression at all until one of them said, "Of course we don't."

And just like that I was dismissed and minutes later my desk was empty and I held my head high as I headed for the elevator and left their office forever.

Good riddance!

~

Two days later I was hundreds of miles away in the lovely place promised by the ad that had caught my attention. The cottage in the picture was rustic and pretty and the ad had promised peace and a tree dotted rural countryside but the price had been beyond my means until it was lowered because no one was interested.

Then it was lowered again. And then again and again until it was in my price range. I'd answered the ad but offered less than it asked because I'm a canny negotiator. My offer was accepted.

Now I was here with a murmuring creek mere

yards from my rented cottage. It was perfect. Quiet and peaceful yet with the internet access that was important to my future and somewhat unusual so far from any large city.

It was a totally rural environment with gravel roads instead of paved ones and a handful of houses scattered about in no particular order near the few stores that made up what must be the town itself.

My immediate thought as I closed the car door and looked around was that the nearby creek was calling to me so instead of checking out my new home I went towards the sound.

The ground was soft from the recent winter thaw with spots of dirty snow in shady places and as I walked towards that murmuring creek my high heels sank in deeply enough that I removed them and walked in my stocking feet. Then I tugged my stockings off, too, and let my toes wriggle in the cold mud as the sound of rushing water became a lovely background to the arguments of a million birds hiding in the huge, old, shade trees just showing the first hint of spring green.

As I drew closer to that murmuring creek I smiled complacently. Yep, I'd done the right thing to drop out of civilization in order to take a few-- or many -- on-line courses to upskill my resume, chat up a few people I'd met online who could connect me with better jobs than the one I'd just left, and generally redirect and restart my career in any city big enough to hold the kind of company that would see my value and never pass me up for promotion. Ever.

I studied the soggy ground ahead of me. The winter thaw wasn't complete but the sun had warmed the exposed soil enough that it wasn't too cold on my bare feet and the squishy mud felt good as I walked far enough to see the creek itself. And then I stopped breathing because what I saw was so perfect that for a moment I didn't believe it was real.

That he was real.

That the tall, dark haired and very, very well-built man in the middle of the creek whipping a line back and forth in the time-tested motion guaranteed to cause the brightly colored, artificial lure on the end of his fly-fishing line to drop precisely in the center of a small, quiet eddy that surely held a trout or two wasn't a figment of my imagination. Or whatever kind of fish swam in the crystal clear water.

He didn't know I was there and I didn't make my presence known. Instead I simply enjoyed the sight. He was poetry in motion. Real life art. The wind ruffled his hair and the surface of the water equally, the sun shone on both man and creek and the budding branches above moved slightly and turned both creek and man into a dance of water and light.

Then a fish struck his line and he played it slowly, patiently, muscles working as he let the line out and then back until he added what looked like a trout to the creel at his waist. I clapped. Startled, he turned towards me.

My breath stopped because he was the guy I'd created in my imagination one piece at a time starting when I was a little girl. Tall, dark hair, and eyes I couldn't make out at that distance, muscles everywhere but not overdone. An outdoor guy, I decided, which description jibed with the fishing gear and the experienced way he'd put his lure exactly where he wanted.

We were standing there like two idiots staring at one another. I stepped closer, holding my high heels in one hand, intending to introduce myself as his head tipped a bit in surprise because he clearly didn't recognize me and, as I thought about it, I realized that in such a small place everyone knew everyone else so my appearance must be a shock not to mention that I was still wearing clothes more suited to the city than a small town.

I wanted to explain. To get to know someone in my new home. To be friendly because that was probably the way things were done here and to find out if he was real or a figment of my imagination.

I took another step so he could hear me over the sound of the creek. I stepped to the bank of the creek overlooking the rushing water and then still another step onto the ground that was overhanging the creek. It seemed solid.

It wasn't.

The ground gave way beneath me and I found myself falling into that sparkling, clean water. I screamed, a knee-jerk reaction to falling as I dropped into water that was only a few feet deep but was ice cold, probably only recently thawed. I would have screamed again but the cold stole my breath.

Before I could get my bearings a hand grabbed my arm and pulled me upright. My hero was inches from me, fly rod in one hand and me in the other, inspecting my wet body. Then I started to shiver.

"You're cold," he said unnecessarily. I wrapped my arms around myself but it did little good. I felt like I'd been dumped naked into a snowbank in the middle of winter. "We need to get you warm." He looked around. "Let's get you into the sunshine. That'll help. And I believe you need my shirt more than I do."

He steered me out of the creek with his one free hand and headed us both towards the sunshine that surrounded my new rental cottage. As soon as we left the shade of the trees that arched over the creek and kept the last vestiges of winter snow intact in small, protected spots I felt warmer. Somewhat.

"Thanks." I was so cold I could barely speak as I shivered uncontrollably. He divested himself of the creel around his waist and started to remove his shirt. "Not necessary," I managed as I shivered harder but was still marginally able to talk.

I pointed to the cottage. "It's mine, at least for the summer." I had to stop speaking momentarily as a severe wave of shivering swept through me but it subsided enough that I could speak once more. "At least it will be when I go inside." I pointed to my car. "I have all kinds of clothes." I looked at him. "I'll be fine." Another shiver, worse than the last, stopped my speech for a moment. "And thanks."

Then as the sun did its work and I knew I'd survive I added before another bout of shivering caught hold of me. "You were awesome back there."

His face lit up as his eyes still swept my soaking self from top to bottom and back again. "You fly fish?"

"I used to. A million years ago with my grandfather. Not since then, though." No place to fish in the city.

The shivering returned and this time it was more violent and lasted longer. He stopped sizing me up and said, "I'll help carry your stuff in. You can shower to get warm while I bring in your bags."

I should have said I could do it myself. I'm totally capable of carrying a few suitcases. But I didn't. Instead, I said, "Thanks," and headed for the door of my rental cottage with my arms still wrapped around my sopping, frozen body.

I started to insert the key but stopped at his chuckle. "It's not locked." I turned to him in surprise. "No place here is locked." He shrugged and well-developed muscles moved in his shoulders. "No reason to lock anything in Southfork."

I pushed the door open and stepped inside and hoped I'd not drip enough that I'd have to mop the floor because I didn't know if a mop or even a broom came with the place. I decided I could use a towel. I'd brought several of those.

He'd already grabbed two suitcases and followed me inside. "So Mrs. Sanders actually rented this place." His voice said he was surprised.

"I watched the ad for weeks. When the rent dropped to my budget I called and offered even less." Said between shivers.

"And she took it and was happy to have someone here for the summer," he said, still chuckling as he looked around for a place to put the suitcases. "She checked out other ads to know what to charge. We told her this isn't the city and that small town, seasonal cottages rent for less. But we couldn't convince her. She thinks people should pay more for places as lovely as Southfork."

"It is beautiful." I wrapped my arms around my shivering body as he deposited my suitcases in the middle of the floor and another bout of shivering overcame me that was the worst yet.

"You should take a hot shower and you should take it now." He pointed to a door. "That's the bathroom. I'll bring in the rest of your things while you thaw."

I grabbed the smaller of the suitcases because it held whatever I'd needed during my trip including a couple changes of clothes and headed for the bathroom and water as hot as I could get it. It wasn't too long before I was luxuriating in a steamy, hot, hot, hot shower.

When I reluctantly got out because if I stayed too long I'd use up all the hot water and get cold all over again I spent an inordinate amount of time toweling myself and getting the knots out of my hair while wondering for the millionth time why I left it long because I went through this same agony whenever it got tangled which was pretty much daily as I wished, also for the millionth time, that I was larger than I am and more in shape because if I was I might not have needed rescuing.

Chapter 2

I exited the bathroom expecting to see all my luggage in the middle of the floor and my savior gone. Instead I saw his back as he stood at the kitchen sink cleaning what looked like a fair amount of fish on a counter covered with old newspapers while whistling a tuneless song.

I stared at him silently because even up close he hadn't lost the appeal I'd felt earlier. If anything it had gone up a notch. He was the kind of guy I'd always wanted to meet and never had. My lower self turned warm just watching those economical, practiced movements.

When he realized I was done with my shower he turned and my insides grew even warmer and fuzzy. "I'd planned on a shore lunch all along so I have all the necessary stuff with me. When I realized there was nothing in this cottage in the way of food I decided to stay here and cook us both some trout." One eyebrow rose in a question. "Is that okay? Almost freezing to death is hard on the body. You need fuel to get warm again."

At that precise moment my stomach rumbled and I said the only thing I could think to say. "That sounds wonderful." Memories of shore lunches with my grandfather brought tears to my eyes but I blinked them away as I wondered at what age I'd forgotten my love of trout streams. And now I had one mere yards from my front door.

I found myself looking forward to a delicious meal

and an hour later I groaned in ecstasy as I pushed away from the table replete with the remains of a shore lunch. During that hour across the table from one another we'd learned a bit about each other because what else would two strangers talk about?

"Susanna Brown." From everywhere because my father's climbing of the corporate ladder had required several moves. And as we ate that delicious trout I explained that I was taking a hiatus from work to upgrade my skills which was why I was in Southfork. I didn't mention that I'd quit my job in a snit of frustration. He didn't need to know that.

"Royce Adamson and I've lived in Southfork all my life." He also mentioned that he was single, a fact I shouldn't have cared about and did. "I make furniture and ship it everywhere." He tipped his head in a direction that I presumed was downtown Southfork. "My workshop is next to the general store."

"Where's the grocery store? I need to do some shopping." Yes he was gorgeous but other things were also important. Like eating.

He frowned. "You should have stopped at a big box store on your way here."

"I didn't think to do so."

Another frown. "The general store doesn't carry groceries because people around here shop in real towns. You know, the kinds of places with enough people to support an actual grocery store."

I groaned. "I hope they have something that'll get me through the next few days." Until I was unpacked and had my bearings and could go elsewhere. "Because I don't even have a box of crackers."

His eyes – brown with tiny flecks of gold now that

I was close enough to see – were sympathetic. "Some of the ladies in town get together to make a grocery run once a week but I think they went yesterday so they won't go for a while."

"I can drive." I'd got to Southfork by myself, hadn't I?

His head tilted a bit. "I don't go with the ladies. I take my truck, most of us bachelors do, and we go shopping for everything we can possibly need or want whenever we need enough stuff to make the trip worthwhile. More efficient than weekly." I guessed that kind of shopping might be a guy thing as he continued. "I'm running out of a lot of stuff so it's about time to go again. If I go tomorrow, want to ride along? The truck will hold both of our stuff."

I started to let him know I was perfectly capable of driving a few miles to another town when I realized I didn't know where that town was or which direction I'd have to take to reach it. I kind of folded into myself. "I'll appreciate the ride."

He nodded. "In the meantime what say you visit me for dinner? It'll be better than starving." I'd not be able to eat a decent meal until that shopping trip. Or to eat anything at all. "My spaghetti is to die for and it's on the menu tonight."

My shoulders sagged as I realized I was about to once more be in this gorgeous man's debt. Okay, maybe not everyone would think he was gorgeous but I did. The physique. The outdoorsy vibe. The general air of competence. "Thanks." Then I asked, "Where do you live? How can I find your house?"

"It's the white two-story building behind my workshop which is next to the general store."

"Can you give me specific directions?"

His eyes went wide. Then he threw his head back and laughed. It was a deep, belly laugh and it was beautiful. "You definitely are from the city, aren't you?"

"Why? What did I say?"

"In Southfork you don't ask for specific directions. Instead you ask what the house looks like and where it is in a general sort of way. Then you simply stand in the middle of the street and look around until you see it." He finished with, "The town is that small. You can see it all from that one spot in the center of town." He thought over his words. "Though to be honest it's not actually a town. Southfork is a village." He thought still more. "Not even a village. A hamlet, maybe?" He scowled because even that wasn't right.

I finished for him. "A crossroads?"

His face cleared. "Yep, that's what Southfork is. A crossroads and one of the loveliest places on Earth."

"I agree," I said slowly remembering the trees meeting over that rippling creek and the sunshine and the tiny, quaint cottage that would be mine for as long as I chose.

We cleaned up the lunch dishes and then Royce left so I could unpack. But before leaving, he dug into his supplies and handed me a box of cookies and some grapes. "I brought them for snacks but I think you need them more than I do." He saluted as he headed for the door. "So I'll leave you to settle in." He glanced about. "In this tiny cottage it shouldn't take long."

He was right. Everything was put away in less than an hour during which I'd also made a mini-office in a corner using a wobbly table that had been on the back porch that was usable with a block of wood under one leg to stabilize it. I arranged my things on the top with my laptop precisely in the center. A perfect setting for upgrading my skill sets through online courses. Then I set about finding the internet connection the ad for the cottage had promised so I could sign up for those courses.

I didn't find it.

Maybe Royce Adamson could help. I decided to ask when I went to his place for a dinner that, now that I thought about it, would be very welcome. I finished the snacks and looked forward to tomorrow when I could fill my cupboard with food.

In jeans and a comfortable shirt and wearing a jacket and sneakers that wouldn't sink into the soft earth I spent the hours until that meal outside. I checked out the creek that I now treated with respect from a safe distance. The fields stretching away and into the distance that were dotted with trees and bushes budding out in the warm sun. In mere days, if the sun continued hot, the area would be a green paradise.

I walked the length of the crossroads or town or whatever it was and checked out the few stores, lingering in the single tourist-oriented one and talking with the owner, a solid looking woman who was at home in this rural environment and who informed me I'd sadly misread the ad if I thought it meant the internet connection was dependable.

"Southfork does have internet so the ad was truthful," she said over her glasses after introducing herself as Lottie, no last name given. Because I wasn't local? "We have internet when whatever it is that makes it work actually functions and the wind is from the right direction. It's good enough for most of us because we're pretty laid-back around here. If it doesn't work on Monday, maybe it will on Tuesday. Or next week."

My heart sank. "What about those who need a reliable connection?"

She laughed. "They either pay a fortune or figure out something else to do with their time." Even without checking I knew I couldn't afford dependable service. So how was I to take those online classes? My heart sank as I feared I'd have to say good-bye to both my upskill ambitions and those professional friendships I'd carefully nurtured and planned to continue online so they could help me land a job when I was ready to reenter the world of work.

One thing went well during my explorations. Royce had told the truth about finding his house – or any house – easily by standing in the center of town and looking around. His was clean and neat and larger than expected. It had been built for a family instead of a bachelor and was placed a short distance behind an equally neat workshop and beneath old trees with spreading branches with what might be a garden plot behind it though it was still too early in the year for it to be more than a black rectangle enclosed by a ten foot high fence.

He answered on the first knock. "Don't bother to knock next time. Just come inside and holler. If I'm home I'll answer. If not I'm in the shop. Or somewhere." Wearing snug-fitting jeans and an equally snug-fitting tee shirt, but barefoot. For some reason the combination did things to my insides that I tried to ignore and hoped he didn't notice.

To cover my embarrassment I blurted out the first thing that came to my mind. A question. "Why do you have a high fence around your garden?"

He laughed again. "Deer can jump anything under ten feet and those veggies I work so hard for all summer are for me instead of a bunch of greedy deer."

"Oh." My face turned red as he enjoyed the fact that he knew this little piece of rural knowledge that I clearly didn't. Deer could be pests.

His hand at the small of my back turned my insides to jelly and propelled me through the hallway and to the kitchen where a table was set for two and a pot of spaghetti sauce simmered on the stove. Darn the man, anyway, what gave him the right to be so perfect?

As the incredible smell hit me I salivated and hoped he wouldn't go through some kind of rural initiation ceremony before we could eat. Because I suddenly realized I was starved.

He didn't insist on any rituals that delayed dinner and his spaghetti lived up to his earlier boast. When I couldn't eat another bite no matter how much I wanted to I came up for air and conversation. And questions about internet access.

"How far away is the nearest town with internet access?" Because I'd figured a solution to my internet conundrum. "I need it, I can't afford it here and so must drive somewhere else and sit in my car to do online classes." I explained about the upskilling and that the ad for the rental said there was internet access.

He shoved his chair back and balanced on two legs with his entire body aligned and relaxed as he considered me. Those brown and gold eyes took me in from top to bottom and side to side and I once more hoped he didn't notice how he affected me. "Obviously you need more internet access than most people around here."

"So how far do I have to drive to get it?"

"Fifty miles more or less." I groaned and would have dropped my head to the table and pounded it a few times if I was alone but even without such a gesture it was obvious I was unhappy. He considered me still more. "I have excellent access through a wonderful and very expensive satellite provider. I need it in my business because my customers are all over the country. I'll be happy to share. No charge because we are neighbors."

"You'd do that?" My eyes went wide as I carefully didn't ask what my share would cost if I paid because I undoubtedly couldn't afford it. "Really?"

"It'll be nice to know I'm finally getting my money's worth." He pointed through the window. "It's in the shop, though, so you'll have to share space with a lot of wood."

"Sawdust?" My laptop wouldn't like that.

"My computer is in the office and I keep the door tightly closed and there's an air filtration system." His head tipped much like it had when he was fly-fishing. "It's a rather large office. Space won't be a problem."

"If you'll let me know what hours you're open I'll make sure to be there during those hours and finish well before quitting time."

He held up a finger and shook it at me. "Remember what I said? No one in Southfork locks their doors so you can follow whatever schedule you choose." He thought a moment. "Besides, I don't have regular hours. What if the trout are biting or the garden needs tending?" He finished with, "I refuse to be a slave to a clock or calendar." A decided snort said what he thought of schedules.

"Oh." What else was there to say? And why couldn't I come up with a better response than that single, innocuous word? And why did I have the feeling my well-planned life was about to spin out of control in this tiny hamlet that was home to one of the best-looking men I'd ever seen and where life was lived in a way I could hardly imagine?

Chapter 3

We went shopping the next day. I bought way more than I expected to use in a month and ignored Royce's almost smile at the amount. I knew he was keeping silent so as to let me figure out for myself that when you live in the country you stock up when you can and you buy a lot and that meant different amounts for different people.

But eventually he couldn't keep silent any longer so he pretended a love of cooking might be why I bought so much. "You must like to cook." Then he added in a voice low enough that he hoped I wouldn't hear, "Country living isn't like being in the city. No stores open twenty-four seven if you forgot something." He smiled brightly, thinking I'd not heard as he put still another of my purchases in his truck.

I matched his bright smile with one of my own and ignored the remark about stocking up, choosing instead to let him think I'd only heard the one about cooking. "I do like to cook but the results definitely aren't gourmet." The only truthful thing I could say because my kitchen skills would never match his excellent spaghetti.

Then something occurred to me. "Speaking of which, I owe you a meal. Two meals, actually. Lunch and dinner." Because that's what he'd given to me. "What about lunch tomorrow at my place?" Surely I could come up with something to equal that trout lunch. Anything. I'd brought a cookbook. There must be meals in it somewhere that even a mediocre cook like me could master and I'd figure out the second meal later.

He considered the offer. "Okay but you must take into consideration that the trout are hitting. So what say I stop by as soon as I catch my limit?"

My brain started working on a menu that could come even close to his fresh fish lunch. Then I realized what he'd said. He was willing to come only *after* he caught his limit? Really? And when was that likely to be?

More to the point, what could I serve that could wait for him to finish fishing and it would still be edible? I almost barfed at the challenge but I wasn't about to let him know I was panicking because maybe this was how small towns worked and I'd just have to adapt.

As I tried to figure out menus and how to avoid him seeing how he was affecting me because I'd not only have to cook a few meals for him, I'd have to sit across the table from him while we ate and then again while I worked in his shop, his eyes narrowed.

"Speaking of fishing, you said you fly fish." I nodded. "Do you have a rod?" I shook my head and he continued, "I have several and an extra creel." Of course he did, all dedicated fly fishermen do. My grandfather had six.

"But it's way too cold to go wading now and the shore is unreliable – as you learned yesterday – so you shouldn't fish from there. You might want to get a pair of waders while we're here." He finished with, "There's a sporting goods store in the next block." Then he added, "If you want to do some fishing while you're here."

We headed for that sporting goods store and when

we exited I had a pair of waders plus an assortment of warm things to wear with and inside of them because though the sun was doing its best there was still snow in shaded places and the creek would still be icy.

"Want to practice casting before we head to the creek?" he asked a few days later after a lunch of hamburgers grilled on the ancient grill that came with my cottage because I'd decided I could cook them after he arrived, whenever that would be, and even I couldn't mess up hamburgers.

The meal was a success. I felt like I'd passed a test though I wasn't sure if it was a rural life test or one to determine if I was fit to become a Royce Adamson groupie. "Want to practice a few dry land casts before we head for the creek?" He added, "The trees meet overhead over the creek and it can be tricky to get your line where you want it without getting it stuck in a branch."

"Yes, please." I spoke in a small voice, remembering my grandfather and my childhood. The streams I'd fished with my grandfather had been wide open. No trees anywhere. "I need the practice. It's been years."

We found an open spot behind the cottage in one of those fields that seemed to go on forever. He watched as I pulled a length of line from the reel, dropped it on the ground beside me and tried to remember everything I'd been taught. My mouth went dry as I sent out my first cast. It was a disaster and I was glad for the open field.

But it didn't take long to regain the rhythm of fly fishing and soon Royce decreed my ability equal to his. It was a nice lie but I felt adequate to the creek and the huge, ancient trees that overarched it. So we pulled on our waders and headed for the icy waters of the quiet south fork of the white-water river that came from an unknown place beyond the other side of town and that, after passing my quaint cottage, headed out towards some equally unknown place far, far away.

Royce pointed out a likely spot for me before moving far enough downstream that our lines wouldn't become entangled. I proceeded to cast, watching him covertly during that quiet moment while my fly rested on the water before starting to reel it in, and that was how I figured out what was truly behind his choice of a spot for me.

The bottom of the creek where I stood was level with a sandy bottom. Totally safe. Royce, on the other hand, stood among rocks and threaded his way carefully along an uneven, gravelly creek bed. The man was making sure I'd not end up head first in the cold water as when we'd met while he fished the more dangerous rocky portion. Which also happened to be the most likely spot to find trout.

I didn't know whether to laugh or cry. When we took a break, I let him know I'd seen through his tactic. "It's a good thing we didn't bet on who'll catch the most trout."

"What are you talking about?"

"You gave yourself the premier spot. If we'd have made a bet, I'd lose."

His face turned pink but he didn't look away. "It's also the most difficult spot on the creek to walk. It's not actually safe." The pink became red. "I was considering your safety."

"Or you wanted to catch the most trout. But I'm

letting you know that the time I fell in the creek was an anomaly. I'm usually able to navigate difficult terrain just fine."

"Then when we go back to the creek, we'll switch places."

So we did and I soon wished I'd kept silent because he was right. The rocky bottom was treacherous and I spent so much time being careful not to fall that I caught nothing, not one single trout, while Royce caught his limit.

His grin when we compared catches was infuriating and I'd have said something except I'd asked for it. He shut his creel with a satisfied snap. "Up for another trout lunch?" I nodded and he asked, "Your place or mine?"

"You have a better kitchen." Which he did, the large, white house having been designed for a family with a kitchen that could feed a passel of assorted kids plus numerous relatives and a half dozen or so neighbors.

He agreed. "The cottage is just that. A cottage. A pretty place beside the creek but it was never intended to be a year-around home so no reason for a decent kitchen." Or decent much of anything else, I thought, considering what I now knew was a pretty, quaint, and fairly decrepit cottage in the country. But I loved it in spite of the mice, the wind blowing through cracks in the walls and all the other things that were less than perfect.

Halfway through our lunch, I thought of something. "Does this mean I still owe you two meals because, even though I made one lunch, I haven't yet had you over for dinner and now this lunch adds still another meal to my debt?"

"We both worked on this meal so this one is a draw. You only owe me one meal and I intend to hold you to it."

Preparing the lunch had been an oddly intimate thing with Royce showing me where everything was located and the two of us working in tandem as if we'd done it a thousand times before. There was an element of warmth and something else I couldn't describe added to his pure, unadulterated, sex appeal.

But the meal debt needed to be dealt with. I spoke before I could chicken out. "Tomorrow night." Then I took a deep breath and added, hoping I wasn't displaying a total lack of small-town etiquette by mentioning a specific time. "And it doesn't matter what a bunch of fish are doing. Be at the cottage at six sharp." I frowned sternly. "No later, whether the trout are biting or not." And I waited for him to be shocked by my cavalier disregard of his non-schedule and tell me where to go.

Instead, he said, "Yes ma'am."

"No argument?"

"No ma'am."

He sighed hugely at my surprise and explained. "My momma taught me never to argue with a woman when she gives an actual order. Just say 'yes ma'am' and do whatever she says." His pained expression said it might be hard to follow that advice. "Even if the trout are biting."

I laughed. Couldn't help it. Soon he was laughing with me and I followed him to his back porch that overlooked a yard that was fuzzy green with early spring grass and a garden that was still a black rectangle. He examined that black space. "Want to share my garden? I might have been a bit overly ambitious when I made it so big. I'll never use the full space."

"I suppose so." But honesty is a virtue. "I've never gardened before."

"Why not?"

"Never lived where we could have one." A deficit of having an ambitious father. Choose a house near work to cut commute time with the resulting small to nonextant yard.

He whistled. "Well, if you're up for it, it's easy enough. What do you want to grow?" I didn't know. "Tomatoes? Beans? Squash?"

"Those vegetables sound ominous. And difficult." Best to remind him I was a beginner. "Whatever's easiest."

He blinked. "Radishes in the spring." He'd probably never heard of a beginner gardener because everyone in small towns knows how to grow things, it being a sacred part of their heritage. "When we see how well you do with radishes, we'll decide on other veggies for later."

The silence lengthened and that feeling I got whenever I was near him increased exponentially. It wasn't uncomfortable, though, and it was evolving into something different from that first time I'd seen him. Instead of being firmly planted in the world of sun and earth and sky I felt as if I was suspended between two other worlds and I didn't know which was the real one, the world from before meeting him or the one after. It was an odd feeling, one I'd never experienced and I knew at last what people meant when they said they'd lost touch with reality.

"Thanks for both the fishing and the lunch." I prepared to leave.

Those brown-gold eyes turned to me. The gold flecks I'd never seen in anyone else, ever, were bright pinpricks in brown depths. "It's early yet. Why don't you bring your computer and stuff over to the shop now and we can carve out a spot for you?"

Then those brown-gold eyes darkened and the gold flecks grew brighter. He leaned against the porch rail in what was outwardly a casual way and yet in some way I couldn't figure it wasn't casual at all as my breath left me because somehow I knew those worlds I was suspended between were about to merge.

As I turned to go get my things to bring back to his shop he straightened and took a step towards me. He took my hand in his and turned me around so instead of my leaving we faced one another. Then he wrapped his free hand around my neck and gently pulled me towards him. And kissed me.

Hi again,

I hope you enjoyed the beginning of *Keeping Susanna Safe*. It will be available on Amazon, free with Kindle Unlimited, and a pittance without.

www.ingramcontent.com/pod-product-compliance
Lightning Source LLC
Chambersburg PA
CBHW070420310726
48977CB00003B/769